GL 4-6

QUANAH PARKER

Chief Quanah Parker. (Courtesy of the Panhandle-Plains Historical Museum, Canyon, Texas)

QUANAH PARKER

Comanche Chief

Rosemary K. Kissinger

PELICAN PUBLISHING COMPANY
Gretna 1991

Library of Congress Cataloging-in-Publication Data

Kissinger, Rosemary K.
    Quanah Parker: Comanche chief/Rosemary K. Kissinger.
      p. cm.
    Includes bibliographical references.
    Summary: A fictionalized biography of the last great
Comanche chief, who was the son of a Comanche chief and
Cynthia Ann Parker, a white settler abducted by the
Comanches as a child.
    ISBN 0-88289-785-3
    1. Parker, Quanah, 1845?-1911—Juvenile fiction.
[1. Comanche Indians—Juvenile fiction. 2. Parker, Quanah,
1845?-1911—Fiction. 3. Comanche Indians—Fiction.
4. Indians of North America—Fiction.] I. Title.
PZ7.K67118Qu 1991
[Fic]—dc20
                               90-23036
                                 CIP
                                  AC

Manufactured in the United States of America

Published by Pelican Publishing Company, Inc.
1101 Monroe Street, Gretna, Louisiana 70053

To my dear family and dear friends,
with grateful appreciation
for their unwavering faith and support.

Contents

Acknowledgments

I would like to acknowledge with gratitude those authors who have so kindly allowed me to quote or paraphrase from their previously published material, and I extend special appreciation to the wonderful editors at Pelican Publishing Company who so patiently lent their expertise towards the publication of this book.

Introduction

Quanah Parker was the son of a Comanche chief and a white woman who had been abducted as a child from a Texas fort.

At the time of Quanah's mother's abduction, the Comanches were at the height of their power. Nearly 20,000 strong, they ranged throughout Texas and into adjacent states.

But the picture began changing as more and more white settlers migrated west. They built on, fenced in, and tilled for farming the Indians' traditional hunting grounds.

As a youth, Quanah watched the changes the white men brought. He saw timber cut, the grazing lands farmed, barbed wire strung. As a result, buffalo and deer herds began to disappear, and with them the Indians' central source of food, warmth, and housing. As he grew, he became ever more determined to fight the invaders.

When he became a young chief, his was the most feared band of the Great South Plains. His Quahadis Comanches plagued half of Texas with attacks on frontier settlements. His name was spoken in awe, his deeds recounted across the length and breadth of Texas.

The U.S. Army was called upon to force the Indians onto reservations. But neither the army nor the Texas Rangers could contain Quanah's elusive band.

In the end, it was not the army who brought Quanah's band to their knees. It was the greedy hunters, who denuded the land of buffalo, the Indians' primary source of sustenance. The once indomitable chief was faced with the fact that his people were starving and freezing to death.

The last Comanche chief to do so, Quanah reluctantly led his people into Fort Sill, Oklahoma, to surrender. True to his word, Quanah never again went on the warpath. Instead, the young chieftain became an engineer of peace between the red and the white people. He set an example for his people, encouraging them to learn to live in the white man's world, yet always remaining a liaison between their past and their future.

He became a friend of three United States presidents, who came to know and admire his integrity and values, and he earned the everlasting gratitude of both the red and white nations.

CHAPTER 1

The Attack on Fort Parker

May 1836

It was hot and humid and midday. A large war party composed mainly of Kiowa and Comanche Indians surrounded a small log fort in South-Central Texas. They were hidden from view by a thick forest of pine trees.

Faces garishly painted, their long black hair in braids adorned with ribbons and feathers, the Indians sat quietly on their similarly decorated mustangs. The leader of the raid surveyed their target with cold, calculating black eyes.

Inside the stockade, seven small cabins housed families who had recently migrated from Illinois. The largest clan, under the leadership of Elder John Parker, had made the hazard-filled journey in an effort to bring the message of the Baptist church to the frontier.

The new emigrants had erected the tall log fort earlier in the spring and settled into a pattern of productivity. Most of the men left the fort early each morning to cultivate small farms they maintained in the vicinity where the soil was rich, the vegetation lush. Nearby the Navasota River furnished clear water and abundant fish, while the surrounding countryside abounded in wild game. The men who remained in the fort for the protection of the women and children busied themselves with the daily chores of caring for the few animals and horses kept inside. Some of the women were making lye soap, some were churning butter, and some were busily making cheese.

Since there had been no hostile Indian activity in the vicinity in recent months, the fort's main gate had been left open in hopes of catching any cooling breezes from the river.

It was young Benjamin Parker's turn, that day, to stand guard at the gate. Languidly he leaned against it, wiping sweat from the open neckband of his homespun shirt with a large, wrinkled calico handkerchief. His rifle rested against the rough pine wall, within arm's reach.

Just inside the gate, Ben's father, the Elder John Parker, paused briefly in his chores to talk with his wife, "Granny," as she sat on the top step in front of their cabin, shelling early peas for their dinner.

Farther along the line of cabins, in the sparse shade offered by a corner of the yard, their nine-year-old, blond, blue-eyed granddaughter, Cynthia Ann, cradled her rag doll in her arms and crooned to it. "Lullaby, baby dear. Close your eyes, baby dear . . . " she sang softly. At her side, her seven-year-old brother, John, valiantly tried his hand at whittling, intent upon making a whistle from the reed his father had brought back from the river bottom that morning.

The day had begun with a tranquil sameness, the occupants of the fort unaware of the danger lurking only a few hundred yards away, just inside the treeline where the Indian war party watched and waited.

Then, at a silent signal from their leader, three young braves kneed their ponies' ribs, urging them forward, and paced slowly toward the fort. One carried a dirty white cloth on the end of his lance. As they emerged from the cover of the trees, Ben's startled glance caught their approach. He sounded the alarm with the dread cry of "Indians!"

Activity in the yard froze. All eyes turned toward the gate. Ben reached for his rifle. "I'll see what they want," he called over his shoulder. "Perhaps only food . . . " he said hopefully, eyeing the white flag. He cradled his rifle casually under one arm, hoping to project a picture of readiness as well as the spirit of peace and friendship. With a smile he strode forward to meet the approaching Indians.

His brother, Silas, grasping the axe with which he had been chopping kindling wood for Granny's cooking fire, rushed toward the gate to join Ben but his father stopped him. "Wait," he said. "Let Ben speak with them. They seem to mean us no harm. There are only three—and they carry the white flag." Neither he nor the others could see the Indians still hidden by the trees.

The three young warriors walked their ponies slowly toward Ben, then arced, circling him. A closer look at their painted faces told Ben this was not just another hunting party. Too late he realized the white flag was merely a ruse. Realizing the danger, he tried to stall for time so that those inside the fort could prepare for whatever was to come.

Silas and Elder John, watching from just inside the gate, caught words of pidgin English as Ben attempted to communicate with the trio who had surrounded him, touching him lightly, tauntingly, with their lances. "Counting coup," Indians called it—a game supposed to prove bravery—approaching close enough to touch an enemy. Then, it ceased to be a game! Suddenly one of them lunged forward, stabbing Ben with his arrow-sharp lance. The other two did the same, repeatedly, until their three spears dripped with his blood. Ben's eyes clouded with pain, then closed forever as he slumped to the ground.

Shrieking wildly, brandishing their bloody lances, the Indians wheeled their ponies and burst into the fort before the stunned occupants could fasten the big gate against them. A hail of arrows flew as the redskins surged into the courtyard, followed by the horde from behind the trees.

In the frenzy that followed, five men from the fort were slain, among them, Elder John. Granny Parker was pinned to the ground with a lance in her shoulder. She would survive. Silas would not; his body riddled with arrows. Nor would Samuel

Frost and Robert, his teenage son. Her doll and his unfinished whistle lying forgotten at their feet, Cynthia Ann and John stared in horror from their corner of the yard.

As the first cry of "Indians!" reached her, Cynthia Ann's mother rushed to the door of their cabin. In one fleeting instant, her eyes took in the panorama of death and destruction, seeing her husband lying among those slain. Clutching her little son, Silas, Jr., by the hand and carrying baby Orlena in her arms, she called urgently to Cynthia Ann and John, "Children! Come quickly!"

She was shepherding her children hurriedly toward a small gate at the rear of the fort when two of the mounted Indians caught sight of the fleeing family and turned their ponies to overtake them. One scooped up Cynthia Ann and flung her across the mane of his horse while the other leaned down and grabbed the screaming, struggling John.

"Mother! Mother!" the children cried as they were borne away. It was the last time the mother would see either of them. Herding the few horses from the fort's animal enclosure, the Indians fled.

Alerted by the sound of gunfire and the sight of smoke, the men who had been a distance away in the fields raced back to the fort, fearing in their hearts they would find disaster.

What they found was worse than anything they had imagined; the fort was a shambles, with mutilated bodies strewn about, cabins gutted by fire . . . and the screams of two terrified children growing fainter as the marauders disappeared back among the trees.

CHAPTER 2

Abducted !

The war party, with its young captives and the stolen horses, crashed through the woods, no longer concerned with the need for silence. They headed back to their stronghold in the faraway Staked Plains of West Texas.

Terrified, Cynthia Ann, crushed between the strong arms of her captor, clung to the mane of his coal-black racing pony. She realized that if she lost her grip and fell, she would be trampled by the dozens of Indians she could hear thrashing along in their wake.

Occasionally she caught sight of her brother, John, his face tear-streaked, his corn-colored hair flopping as he bounced along on another pony, firmly in the grasp of the redskin who had abducted him.

Flayed by thorns and branches, the children's arms and legs were soon bloodied and painful. But grimly they held on while the Indians, following their usual raiding custom, pushed on, putting distance between themselves and any possible pursuers.

For the first hour the raiders took advantage of the camouflage offered by the pine forest. Then they turned due west toward the safety of their desert lair, leaving the pine greenery behind. From then on, they would travel toward the uncompromising heat and desolation of the desert country.

It was well into the night before the Indians finally stopped to make camp. Unceremoniously they dumped their young captives on the ground, binding them hand and foot. They needn't have bothered, Cynthia Ann thought. We couldn't attempt to escape, even under the cover of darkness. Which way could we go? And on foot? Both she and John were so battered and bruised by the dash through the underbrush and the unaccustomed grueling ride, they were reeling, in a state of shock, from pain and hunger and fright.

For the first time since their capture, Cynthia Ann found herself close enough to her brother to speak to him as they lay hobbled side by side. "John," she whispered through the darkness. "We must be brave. Someone will come for us. Someone will save us."

But even as she spoke, her mind silently questioned who? for hadn't she seen her father lying dead at the fort, Elder John slain, and Uncle Ben . . . she shuddered and tried to push the still vivid pictures from her thoughts. She only knew she must remain Big Sister, and look out for John, not letting him sense her fears. "Be a brave boy," she whispered before a threatening glare from one of the Indians ended her attempt at conversation.

A campfire was built and the men gathered around, roasting something over the flames, the tone of their voices and the laughter that ensued indicating a pent-up excitement and camaraderie they had not exhibited during the long hours of the ride. When they had finished eating, Cynthia Ann saw her captor rise from the circle and walk toward her, a large bladed knife in hand. She cringed as he turned her roughly on her side and brought the knife down. With one slash he cut the cord that bound her hands and thrust a piece of almost raw meat into them. Hunger gnawed at her insides but she looked with disgust at the unidentifiable bloody mass in her hands.

John's captor appeared suddenly in their midst, releasing John from his bonds and bringing him a similar slab of food. John eyed the offering briefly. The corners of his mouth turned down, his tongue thrust out over the drawn lips in a grotesque parody of loathing. At another time Cynthia Ann would have giggled at her brother's comic grimace but that night she could not laugh. Not knowing when they would be fed again, she signaled to him to eat, making an attempt herself, silently urging him to join her.

Faced with her own feeling of revulsion, she closed her eyes and took a tentative bite, but her sense rebelled at the taste of seared crusty hide and blood-raw meat. Her stomach knotted and she retched painfully, spitting into the darkness. How long, she wondered, could she and John survive without food, for surely they could never eat the Indians' fare.

With nightfall, a cool breeze had risen. Cynthia Ann pulled her tattered skirt closer about her legs and turned toward the fire although she was too far away to derive much benefit from its warmth.

The warriors, their hunger satisfied, leaped up, one by one, circling the campfire, dancing with wild shrieks and defiant gestures, singing of their victory at the fort, brandishing the new scalps on their lances.

Exhaustion overtook Cynthia Ann and she slept while their shadows twirled and twisted in the firelight. Mercifully she did not see her brother being bartered away later that night as the Indians split their loot from the raid and the tribes parted company. Nor did she hear if he cried out as he was wrenched away, disappearing into the night with one of the smaller bands.

At sunup, Cynthia Ann was tugged rudely awake and again swung up onto her captor's horse. This time, however, she was put up behind him. She felt hesitant about touching him, bare as he was to the waist, wearing only a breechclout and moccasins. She wondered desperately how she could hold on when the horses began to gallop. At the first spirited movement of the horse, she decided! She threw both arms around the Indian's waist and held on tightly!

For another full day the band, considerably smaller now, pushed farther out into the hot, sandy desert of the Texas panhandle. The landscape, almost barren now from horizon to horizon, was dotted with occasional vicious-looking spiny cacti, some growing almost as tall as the horses' heads. Stinging sand, flung by a constant wind, pelted Cynthia Ann's once fair skin, now burned scarlet and pocked by sun blisters.

After several days of riding, Cynthia Ann noticed the terrain begin to change. Short buffalo grass appeared, growing abundantly, tempting the horses whose heads had to be reined up sharply to keep them from slowing the pace by munching along the way. The ponies danced about on light feet, no longer disciplined to a steady hard ride. The men, too, grew more exuberant, loosing their steeds to sudden bursts of speed, racing each other for miles with whoops, waving wildly to their companions until the others caught up, joking, making fun among themselves. Only Cynthia Ann's captor refrained from the games, apparently afraid he would unseat her.

Suddenly all of the horses cantered to a slow walk, then halted, altogether, abruptly, standing still, stiff-legged. Cynthia Ann peeped around from behind her captor. What she saw caused her to gasp and grasp the Indian's waist more tightly. They were poised on the edge of a cliff!

Below them, strung out alongside a stream, was a large Indian encampment. That explained it, she realized—the excitement of the men and their horses—they had known they were almost home! A matching wave of excitement rose to meet them as the women in the camp celebrated the return of their men.

Carefully the horses picked their way down the slender path along the canyon wall. From the lodges, spaced between prickly pear trees and tall cottonwoods, Cynthia Ann watched women and children and old men emerge. The brown-skinned, half-bare children ran about the camp, exhilarated, filled with expectation, anxiously awaiting stories of the warriors' far-off raid. Single file, the braves walked their horses through the camp, Cynthia Ann's captor in the lead.

More frightened now than at any time since her capture,

Cynthia Ann clutched her captor's waist even tighter as she watched with fascination the scene unfolding before her eyes. There were racks of meat drying in the sun, skins of animals stretched for curing, a few old men sitting on buffalo robes outside their tipis enjoying their smokes in the sun, scroungy-looking dogs skulking among the dwellings, and women running alongside the horses, greeting their men.

Everyone stared at the strange white child with her long blond hair and big blue eyes. Cynthia Ann stared back, eyes wider than usual. Her captor halted before the tipi of a kindly looking, brown-skinned older woman whose round cheeks were touched by a faint smile.

"Grandmother-Walks-On-Wind," the young warrior addressed her formally.

"Peta Nocona," she acknowledged him just as gravely.

"I bring you the gift of a girl-child to ease your days alone," he said. Reaching back, with a strong arm, he deftly deposited Cynthia Ann at the grandmother's feet. Then he was gone, riding off to his own lodge, without a backward glance.

Walks-On-Wind squinted down at the young captive for a long moment, studying the frightened child trembling before her, seeing the fringe of tears that clung to Cynthia Ann's pale lashes.

"Come. Come," she said kindly in her own tongue, gesturing, relying on sign language to help the child understand her meaning.

Cynthia Ann Parker had no way of knowing, but at that moment she was beginning her education into the Comanche way of life, the only life she would know for the next twenty-four years.

CHAPTER 3

Comanche Bride

Eight years later, she stood quietly but confidently in Grandmother-Walks-On-Wind's tipi, as two of her Comanche "sisters" helped her dress for her wedding.

She was now thoroughly Comanche, having long since forgotten her own language and her Anglo past. Her pale blond hair had darkened; her skin, once so fair, was now tanned from years of exposure to the harsh weather of the plains. Only her blue eyes remained a constant reminder of her difference from the tribe that had adopted her as one of its own people. Grandmother-Walks-On-Wind had named her Naudah.

As the sisters gathered around her, Grandmother watched the preparations. Observing the dreamy look in those blue eyes, she sighed, "That is the way a girl should look on her wedding day," and prophesied it would be a happy marriage.

Naudah had risen early that morning and bathed in the river, anointing her skin with one of Grandmother's soothing lotions. Then, as the sun tinged the sky with its first rosy rays, she lifted her palms in supplication, offering a prayer to the Spirit-Who-Brightens-The-Day: "May I be a good wife to my husband," she asked. "May I bear him healthy children—many sons to follow his path."

Back in Grandmother's tipi, she stepped into the soft blue-beaded moccasins she had especially prepared for that day. She held up her arms and the sisters slipped her wedding dress over her head. That, too, she had made. The soft deerskin settled over her hips and she smoothed the dress in place. The sisters exclaimed as they examined the matching blue beading she had worked into an intricate starburst at the neckline.

"The design is her own," Grandmother told them proudly.

"But it was Grandmother who taught me beading," Naudah hurried to say, adding wistfully, " just as she taught me many things through the years, preparing me for this day!"

She caught Grandmother's eye and felt that she, too, was remembering the day, eight years earlier, when, as a frightened young captive, Cynthia Ann had stood before her . . .

Walks-On-Wind had beckoned the child into her tipi. With kind, calm gestures, she had taken the tattered calico dress from the little girl and had washed her dirt-encrusted body and her tangled, sweat-streaked hair. On the scratches and scrapes she had smoothed a sweetly aromatic salve, made from her own herb recipe. Over the tender, sunburned skin she had lathered another mysterious-looking, soothing ointment.

The child had stood timidly, being administered to, learning trust in her new environment, at the hands of the gentle old woman who had been left alone, her sons lost long ago in battles, her daughters long since married. Walks-On-Wind was grateful for Peta Nocona's gift of the young girl and looked forward to her aid and companionship.

Grandmother had taught her Comanche ways . . . sending her with other girls from the village, who would later accept her as a "sister," to gather firewood, to select berries from the forests, to choose the plants and herbs Grandmother needed to make her special lotions. Later she was taught how to prepare animal skins for clothing, how to sew with porcupine quills the softened deerskins, how to bead and fringe.

And, as she grew older, Naudah learned how to put up a lodge made of buffalo skins, and how to take it down when it was time for the tribe to move their homes to follow, for food supplies, the animal migrations. She learned how to pack the travois that would trail behind the sure-footed mules carrying the carefully packed cooking utensils and clothing. Oh, there had been so much to learn!

Eventually the Comanche ways had crowded her Anglo background from her memory. As she grew to be a young woman, she learned to recognize when a young brave became infatuated. She understood when, day after day, a young swain just happened to be at the spring when she came to fetch water, and offered to carry it back to camp for her. Or when a young warrior never took his eyes off her when she rose to join the other girls in their stately, feminine, traditional dances at the campfires. Naudah knew.

But her blue eyes looked past all the suitors and sought out instead, Peta Nocona, the warrior who had abducted her years before. She watched, shy-eyed, each time he returned to camp after one of his long, wandering raids, and worried each time he left with war parties. She rejoiced for him when he was recognized as a leader and chosen as chief of the Noconis band. She knew her Comanche sisters mooned over him, too, and wondered if she stood a chance.

He never seemed to notice her, except in kindness as tribal kin, but almost as though her prayers were answered, he never took a wife. It seemed as if he had been waiting for her to grow up because one day recently he came to Grandmother's tipi with a string of ten fine horses, asking for Naudah as his wife . . .

Coming back to the present from her reveries, Naudah impulsively hugged Grandmother-Walks-On-Wind and her two sisters. Then, following sedately as they pulled aside the door flap of the tipi, she stepped outside of the lodge where Peta Nocona waited for his bride, and put her hand in his.

CHAPTER 4

Quanah Is Born

1845

With the advent of spring, Chief Nocona announced to his tribe that it was time for the Noconis to begin their annual trek northward, seeking a cooler camp in preparation for the coming hot months.

"We will go to the Laguna Sabinas," he decided, intent upon keeping well within the Comanche stronghold of the Staked Plains. His people were happy with his decision, remembering the alkaline lake there in a valley carpeted with flowers. The desert air, they recalled, was scented with the sweet aroma of yellow buttercups and purple violets, the rolling hills bluebonnet-fringed. Previous seasons there had been happy ones.

Naudah, now large with her expected first child, prepared for the migration with happy anticipation. There was always much chattering and camaraderie among the women as they aided each other, lifting down the skins that clothed the tipis, and taking down the tall lodge poles. The earthern pots used for carrying water, and the bowls from which they ate, had to be carefully packed in soft skins for the long voyage over rough terrain. Nearby, mules stood patiently waiting for the long travois poles to be strapped to each side, carrying each family's supplies. With the men riding their favorite mustangs, women and children also mounted, younger boys herding the loose horses, the mules plodding along at the end of the line, the move began.

Once at the new camp, the same enthusiasm prevailed as when they left the last one behind. Lodge poles went up, skins were stretched over them, the sides rolled up for ventilation, and household items were stacked around the side of the tipis. Finally, near the end of the day, with their home once more in order, Naudah began planning her own special project for the next day, the "birthing lodge."

She chose a flat, grassy knoll, isolated from the rest of the camp, high above the lake's edge. This will be where my baby will utter its first cry, will see the first light of day, she thought, contented, standing at the door of the birthing lodge, looking out over the flower-laden valley.

There were not many days to wait for the anticipated event. When she felt the first pangs, she called Grey Gull from her tipi and Moon Girl from hers, and they walked with her away from the camp. Entering the lodge, closing the door flap behind them, Naudah lay down upon the bed of soft skins that she herself had scraped and stretched and prepared in anticipation of the day.

On each side of the bed, two large stakes had been driven deep into the ground. Lashed to these poles were rawhide leather thongs for Naudah to grasp as the hours of labor progressed. At her side, one sister knelt to aid in the birth, while the other tended the fire to keep the mother comfortable and to supply warm water to bathe the newborn infant.

Thus the child of a blond, blue-eyed Anglo mother and an Indian father was born, in primitive Comanche fashion.

Grey Gull exclaimed, "My sister, you have a son!" and held the baby close for Naudah's inspection.

"A strapping son!" Moon Girl chimed in happily.

The blue-eyed mother raised herself on one elbow and leaned closer for her first glimpse of her new son. She reached to smooth the fingers of his tiny clenched fist, and fondled his little toes. "Take him to his father," she told her sisters, wishing she could be there to see his face, but remembering that Comanche custom forbad her leaving the birthing lodge until she was clean and free of the birth signs.

In their lodge in the center of the village, the chief waited expectantly for word of the birth. Within a few hours after Naudah had entered the birthing lodge, the sisters proudly bore the child into Peta Nocona's presence. "You have a son!" they told him respectfully, joy shining in their dark eyes.

The chief took the warm, fur-blanketed little bundle into his arms. Carefully peeling away the cover, he looked down at the lusty-lunged, copper-hued baby. His eyes raised heavenward, he held the child out before him, and thanked the Great Spirit for the safe arrival of his first child.

When the baby was returned to its mother, with great care Peta Nocona painted a large black dot near the door flap of his tipi, announcing to all that he had been blessed with a son. Then he sent word to the Medicine Man that the child must receive a name. That was not always done so soon after a child was born but Peta Nocona was proud of his firstborn son and wanted the naming ceremony to take place immediately. Often days or weeks went by before a name was chosen, but Naudah had asked that the name of their son be taken from the sweet-smelling valley of his birth.

The next morning, as the first rays of the sun touched the rim of sky over the distant hills, the most important men of the village gathered in the chief's lodge, cast in a half-circle around the campfire. The chief faced them, with his son between.

The Medicine Man was the last to enter. Arrayed in his finest plumage and beaded garments, he paid homage to the child who lay contentedly before him, on a rug of soft furs.

Facing east, the Medicine Man drew deeply on his ceremonial pipe and blew the smoke toward the eastern sky. He turned and sent a puff to the north, to the west, to the south. Then, lifting the child, presenting it in the same four directions, he repeated each time, "His name shall be Quanah [Fragrance]. Bless this child," he intoned, "that he may one day become a great chief, like his father!"

CHAPTER 5

Comanche Childhood

As an infant, Quanah looked like a full-blooded Indian. High cheekbones were covered by dark coppery tones of baby fat. His hair was straight and black and his little eyes as dark as currants. The only discernible attribute of his Anglo ancestors became evident after the first few months when his eyes turned a distinct blue-grey.

The first months of his life were spent swaddled in softest buckskin, laced onto a stiff rawhide board that could be strapped comfortably to his mother's back, or laid aside like a cradle, within her arms' reach. Contentedly, he'd lie for hours, listening as his mother crooned Indian lullabies while she went about her chores. Or he would lie quietly, hearing the comforting sound of chatter and laughter as Naudah joined the other women of the village while they scraped the great skins of buffalo for softening, or perhaps were busy slicing long strips of meat to be hung on tall racks for curing. What he liked most of all, though, was when she swung his board on the low limb of a tree near the lake, leaving him to sway happily in the breeze while she bathed and frolicked nearby with her friends.

By the time Quanah was able to sit alone, Naudah had begun training him in balance on horseback, putting him up in front of her in the saddle whenever she rode Southwind, her palomino.

As he grew older, and could understand more, she would talk to him as they rode, training his mind early. The men would take over from there later. "Come," she would say to him. "Feel the power of the horse! One day you will conquer that power. Comanches," she told him with pride, "are the greatest horsemen in the world!" She could have added that the Comanche women rode almost as well as the men for, although trained by mothers and grandmothers and aunts for wifely duties, the girls liked to slip away and practice horseback riding with the boys from the village, usually trying to emulate the boys' more hair-raising feats.

More than once Naudah had returned to Grandmother's tipi with bruises and scrapes gained from falling off a speeding pony whose side she had tried to cling to, pretending to shoot arrows from under the horse's neck at enemy bowmen, the way the older boys and men could do. The boys always hooted with derision at the young girls' attempts but secretly they admired their courage and daring, and in later years would be proud of wives who could ride with them.

Before Quanah was barely five years old, his father chose from his own fine herd of horses, a small, gentle pony his son could ride at his mother's side.

Peta Nocona was often absent from the village, off on forays for food, raiding for horses, trading, or visiting other tribal chieftains. Quanah's education into an Indian boy's way of life was not neglected. Indeed, in the village there were always several grandfathers, too old for long hunts or lightning raids on their enemies, who were happy to take over the early instruction of the boys.

When one of them made Quanah his first small bow and fitted it with blunt arrows, Quanah shouted with glee. "Ai-ee! Now I can be a great hunter!" he cried, rushing off to show his friends, Lone Calf and Blue Eagle, before scampering away to practice on small birds and fat little lizards lazing in the sunshine. As his childish skills sharpened and he was allowed to venture a little farther away from camp, he stalked shy little prairie dogs (who were too fast for him), and sometimes brought home squirrels and rabbits for his mother's stew pot.

Within a few years he graduated to riding young colts bareback with Lone Calf and Blue Eagle and the other boys of his age. Then he was considered old enough to be initiated into the job of herding the horses near the camp. That sometimes seemed to Quanah to be the most boring and menial of chores, but then he realized that one day he and the other boys would finally be allowed to join the men on their raiding parties, and there the herding ability would be useful. On the raid, two or three of the older boys would ride to the half-way point of the raid, where they were left with extra horses while the men rode on. Upon the warriors' return from the raid, they could change from hard-ridden ponies to the fresh horses awaiting them. If they were closely pursued, that change might make the difference between death from the pursuers and an easy escape back to the camp.

By his early teens Quanah had learned to track larger game of the sort that would help feed the entire tribe. With newfound patience and cunning he came to understand the prairie as well as the forest, to make an ally of the wind and the rain, . . . to test his physical endurance. One day, he knew, it would no longer be a game and fun. As a young warrior he must be able to feed not only himself and his family, but all those of his band as well.

From his father, Peta Nocona, and the tribal elders, Quanah absorbed the history of his people. Hearing the legends, there grew within him a fierce pride in his Comanche heritage that would never diminish.

Sitting quietly, respectfully, on the farthest fringe at meetings between his father and the most important men of the village, he learned more and more about the Comanche's most despised enemy, the Texan, who, through the years, had steadily encroached on traditional Indian hunting grounds, felling trees, moving cattle onto buffalo grazing lands, stretching miles of barbed wire. His mother, he knew, was once of the Anglos, but he looked at her with love and respect, knowing she was now thoroughly Comanche and that she, too, hated the Texans who were stealing their lands.

The other children sometimes teased him about his white blood. Even though he understood they were just teasing, Quanah, standing tall and straight in his moccasins and breechclout, chin thrust forward, would vow before them, "When I am chief, I shall raid the Texans every day until they retreat from our land!"

A few years later his father watched proudly as young Quanah returned from his first major hunt, carrying a fine young buck into camp. And he watched with equal pride that night at the celebration around the campfire, when Quanah shared his kill with all of the band—remembering respect for the elders by first presenting the largest portions to the grandfathers who had been his teachers.

And later that night, back in their tipi, Peta Nocona smiled tolerantly as his son pressed him to be allowed to take part in the more exciting, more dangerous buffalo hunts. Remembering his own boyhood days, and his youthful eagerness to prove himself a man, he understood and told Quanah earnestly, "My son, you have become a hunter. You will be an even greater one. But be patient. Your time will come!"

How prophetic his father's words were, for in the next few years the adversities to be visited on Peta Nocona, Naudah, Pecos (Quanah's younger brother) and Prairie Flower (Quanah's baby sister) would fall heavily upon Quanah's shoulders. All that he had learned during his childhood and early adolescent years would be put to the test.

CHAPTER 6

Captive at Pease River

1860

From the time the white settlers had begun invading their homelands, the Indians had fought back with sporadic raids—killing, stealing horses and cattle, and burning farms.

The pioneers had come west with the idea that the land was open and free for the taking. They did not look upon the land as belonging to the Indians. They could not understand the culture of the Indians and their almost reverential feeling for their lands. They did not understand that they were taking away the Indians' food when they fenced off the deer and buffalo. Nor did they understand that the Indians would fight on, to keep from being pushed from their lands.

A new wave of trouble erupted when the Penateka band was driven from their reserves by the Texans. Enraged, Peta Nocona's band joined the other Indian tribes in a backlash determined to discourage Anglos from their further westward push in Texas. Revenge raids erupted on both sides, the battles escalating into an even bloodier war.

The hue and cry among the Texas pioneers already committed to their farms in remote parts of the counties became so strong that young Lawrence Sullivan "Sul" Ross, newly commissioned captain in the Texas Rangers, was instructed to raise a company and go after the Indians. Before, the Rangers had always been called upon after a raid was committed. "Too late," Ross explained. By the time he could muster a force, the raiders were long gone, and in most cases, traces of their route were indistinguishable.

So, joined by incensed volunteers and frontiersmen, Ross formed a company of seventy or so, and rode off. Somewhat to their surprise the Texans located Peta Nocona's camp at Pease River where the chief, not out with a war party or on a raid, but on a buffalo hunt, had brought only a small number from his village.

Unaware of the impending danger, Nocona had left only a few men in the camp with the women and children. Quanah, now a brave of about fifteen years, no longer a novice to the hunt, had ridden out with the men. Young Pecos, Quanah's twelve-year-old brother, excitement aglow in his dark eyes, had joined the hunt for the first time, relegated with three other youngsters his age to packing down the buffalo for return to the Pease River camp.

Naudah, holding her small daughter, Prairie Flower, in her arms, had stood before their tipi and waved as her husband and two sons rode away with the hunting party.

It was midmorning when she emerged from the tipi again. With Prairie Flower in one arm and carrying a water jar in her other, she headed for the lake to fetch water. Suddenly there was a cry of "Anglos!" as a lone rider raced through the camp with the awful alert. Seeing the dust cloud raised by the swift approach of many horses, Naudah dropped the jar and, clutching her child more closely, fled along with the other women toward the trees while the men prepared to defend them.

The mounted men swept into the camp, riding down the Indian men, stampeding among the lodges, wheeling back and forth, the volunteers firing indiscriminately at men, women or children. Only the Rangers seemed reluctant to shoot the fleeing women.

In the melee of racing horses, panic-stricken villagers, and shouted commands, Peta Nocona's longtime Mexican captive,

Joe, appeared at Naudah's side. "Quickly! To the horses!" he yelled above the din. Tucking the child effortlessly under one arm, he guided Naudah, on the run, toward horses staked on the outskirts of the village. If they could just reach the horses, he knew her chances for survival multiplied for she was a strong, able rider.

Joe grasped her arm as she vaulted onto a dappled pony and reached for Prairie Flower. He threw himself onto another horse and followed as Naudah's horse plunged away from the fray. But two riders were almost upon them—Sul Ross and his lieutenant. A shot from the captain's gun knocked Joe from his saddle. Ross waved to the lieutenant to ride on and capture the woman. Meanwhile Ross turned his attention back to Joe who had rolled away from his fallen horse, and, bow and arrow drawn, was firing desperately at the Ranger captain.

When Naudah realized she had no chance of eluding the soldier, and fearing he would kill her child with the rifle he waved over his head as he shouted for her to halt, she slowed her horse and turned to face him. Holding Prairie Flower high so he could see the baby clearly, she pleaded with him not to kill her child.

The lieutenant herded Naudah back to the clearing where the other survivors had been gathered. There were not many. Led past the body of the Mexican, she cried out, "Oh, Nocona's Joe!" The captain, hearing the name of Nocona, and Naudah's anguished wail, assumed it was Chief Peta Nocona he had killed.

Suddenly the lieutenant called to Ross, "Captain, sir! This one's not Indian! She's got blue eyes!" The captain approached the cringing Naudah who turned away from him, hiding her child against her breast.

"You're right, Lieutenant. She's white." He shook his head. "When we get back to camp, we'll have to go over all the reports of captive white women. Maybe we can find her family. If there's any of them left . . . "

In anguish Naudah joined the other women from her camp in their eerie death chant for those who had been slain. Twice

Ross approached her, trying to make her understand that he realized she was white and assuring her that she would be taken care of. But Naudah, who had not spoken her people's language for over twenty years, recognized none of his words.

She was taken, along with other captives, to Camp Cooper where she was separated from the Indian survivors and turned over to a group of sympathetic soldiers' wives, to be bathed and given "proper" clothes. Ironically, twenty-four years earlier a kindly Indian grandmother had taken her tattered calico dress and had dressed her in buckskin. This time, the soldiers' wives took away the buckskin and dressed her in calico.

The day after the tragedy at Pease River, Chief Peta Nocona triumphantly led his men back to camp following a successful hunt. Unaware of the terrible events that had taken place in his absence, he returned with sufficient food to feed his band for months to come, his men pleased with their hunt.

Joy was quickly replaced with stunned horror as the hunters rode into the scene of devastation, finding their camp had been overrun, their people decimated. They saw the burned lodges, and the bodies of men, women and children, their flesh bloodied by gunshot, lying dead where they had fallen in their attempt to escape the massacre.

Quanah slipped haphazardly off his horse, Pecos at his heels, searching frantically among the victims for their mother and little sister. It was soon evident that Naudah and Prairie Flower were not among the dead but had been taken captive.

"Anglos! Soldiers!" the men cried as they examined the tracks churned by blacksmith-shod horses. Those with missing families raced their ponies alongside the retreating tracks, intent upon overtaking the soldiers and rescuing their loved ones. But they had only tracked a short distance from the camp before they found that a violent windstorm the night before their return had wiped out any possibility of following the departing Anglos.

Stoically, the chief, hiding his own grief and anger, recalled the men. "There is nothing we can do for the captives. We must take our dead back to our village for proper burial." Quanah, his steel-grey eyes still hopelessly scanning the far horizon as they rode away, silently vowed vengeance.

Within a short time Quanah suffered further family losses. Pecos died of a fever while still a youngster. His father, the chief, died a little while later from a long-infected lance wound. Now, Quanah, only about fifteen years old, was all alone.

Since an Indian son did not automatically become chief upon the death of his father, Quanah was spared the burden of taking care of a band while he mourned his losses. Disconsolate, he wandered for a time from tribe to tribe, his visits welcomed by the Comanches and Kiowas alike who knew the young brave's story. Eventually, because of his growing prowess as a young warrior, he was invited to join another Comanche band, the Quahadis.

It was not until many years later that Quanah finally learned the true fate of his mother, Naudah, and little sister, Prairie Flower.

CHAPTER 7

The Treaty at Medicine Lodge

1867

With relations between the Indians and the whites worsening, the U.S. government called a treaty meeting at Medicine Lodge Creek in Kansas. Among the Indians who were invited to attend were the Comanches, the Kiowas and the Cheyennes. Most of the tribes sent representatives. Many Comanche bands attended, but the Quahadis with whom Quanah now rode disdained the peace talks and planned to send no one.

Quanah, now a young subchief, intended to boycott the council, too. He distrusted all treaties, feeling that the terms had never meant much in prior years. "Treaties are never kept," he scoffed. However, the young warrior had never been so far north as the Kansas site and was intrigued by the idea of the trip itself. "Also," he told his friends, "I hear the soldiers are bringing gifts for the Indians—beef and sugar and coffee. So, I am going," he said, adding with his ingenious honesty, "...for the gifts!"

He rode north alone, stopping to visit friendly tribes along the way, noting those who had sent emissaries on to the treaty meetings, repeating his own reason for visiting the site. "But I will not sit at the meetings. My band will not vote," he stated firmly.

As he approached the treaty grounds, he was astounded by

41

the gigantic scale upon which the council was laid out. He found row upon row of soldiers' quarters, their guns stacked at the ready in front of each tent. Across the plain, row upon row of Indian lodges faced the soldiers' area. There were many tribes in attendance, he saw. The young brave, fascinated by the elaborate panorama, drifted into the Indian encampment on his mustang, Nightwind. Milling through the network of tribes, he spent the first night among the Cheyennes, reiterating what he had told his own people. "The white man's treaty is good until he wants more land. Then he tells the Indians to move again. The treaty gets changed. It's no good!" He spat in derision.

True to his word, he took no part in the sessions, remaining on the fringe of the meetings, pausing only long enough to hear the white men's words translated.

There were many provisions made for the Indians, he learned, in the proposed treaty. In return for their promise to live on the reservation in peace and never again make war, the Indians would receive a tract of land within the reservation, to be owned exclusively by the family who held it as long as they cultivated it. They would be taught farming, living the white man's way. The Indians would receive, for each man and boy fourteen years of age and older, a suit of clothing consisting of shirt, pants, coat, hat, and a pair of socks. For each woman and girl over the age of twelve, there would be one woolen skirt, twelve yards of calico material, twelve yards of domestic material, and one pair of woolen socks. Those provisions would be dealt to the tribe each October for the next thirty years. In addition, the government would send the Indian children to the white men's schools.

"All of that," the interpreters intoned in appropriate Indian language, in return for the Indians relinquishing their right to occupy any territory outside of the reservation, ever again.

"Our people cannot live that way," Quanah said bitterly, turning away from the meeting in disgust, his feelings of distrust vindicated. In the end, Quanah's band did not sign, but some of the Comanches present did, and the government chose to think that those who did so signed for all. Later they would claim that the Quahadis, and other bands, had broken the treaty by remaining outside the reservation.

On the last night of the council, as Quanah made his way through the maze of tipis, heading back home, he heard his name called from one of the Kiowa campfires.

"Little Belly!" Quanah raised himself and saluted his friend, whom he had not seen for several years, then wended his way toward the Kiowa's tipi. With suspicion he looked down at the young white man with flaming red hair and dark red beard who sat beside Little Belly.

"Quanah," his friend spoke with excitement as he introduced the pair to each other. "Mac has come to the council as an interpreter. He is a friend. And, Quanah, he knows of your mother!"

The words came like a thunderclap. She had not been spoken of in so many years, and Quanah had never expected to hear her name again. The grizzled young man, wearing army blue, with his regulation shirt unbuttoned at the neck for comfort, turned brilliant blue eyes to meet Quanah's stare. "So you are Cynthia Ann Parker's son?" he said.

"Naudah!" Quanah replied. "You know what happened to my mother and my small sister?" he asked incredulously.

Mac made room for Quanah to sit beside him. He rolled himself a cigarette, passing the drawstring bag of tobacco and package of thin paper along to Little Belly on one side and Quanah on the other. Ordinarily Quanah would have welcomed a cigarette but he was too intrigued by the promise of hearing of his mother. He shook his head. Stretching his long blue-clad legs toward the fire, Mac took a puff, and began his story, speaking in the Comanche tongue.

"Just about everyone in Texas," he said, "knows about the little white girl who was captured by the Comanches, and adopted by their tribe, where she lived for nearly twenty-five years."

He looked with compassion at the young Indian who stared at him intently, eagerly drinking in every word. "Now, the way it was told to me," he said, "your mother was taken back by the Texans at Pease River about six or seven years ago. Seeing those blue eyes of hers, they knew right off she was Anglo. The Texas Rangers took her back to Camp Cooper, where she was well treated by army wives while the Ranger captain tried to find her relatives.

"Seems like her Uncle Isaac Parker had never stopped hoping to find her. Over the years he had made many trips, whenever a white woman of about the right age was returned from Indian capture, always hopeful of finding his long-lost niece. Well, he got to Camp Cooper and Captain Ross took him into a room where your Naudah was waiting with one of the army wives. There was also a soldier on guard in the room, as Naudah kept trying to escape.

"Naudah was sitting in a rocking chair, holding her baby. She was wearing a dress given to her by one of the army wives. She couldn't remember any of her own language so she couldn't understand what was happening, and I guess she thought they were going to kill her and her baby. She held tightly to the child whenever anyone was around.

"Well, Isaac came in and looked long and hard at the woman. Her hair was dark blond and her skin was as brown as an Indian's. Nothing like the golden-haired, fair-skinned Cynthia Ann he'd known. He carefully studied her Germanic features and her blue eyes. But when he attempted to come close to her, and speak to her, she cringed and turned away, holding the baby close to her. Uncle Isaac shook his head sadly at the sight of the anguished, frightened woman. But, for the first time in all his encounters with returned captives, he was convinced. Turning to Captain Ross he declared, 'I'm positive! Captain, this woman is my long-lost niece—Cynthia Ann Parker!'

"Hearing her name for the first time since her capture that long-ago day in May 1836, the name struck some small indistinct chord in her memory. She whirled to face him, patting

Quanah's mother, Cynthia Ann Parker, and Quanah's sister, Prairie Flower. (Courtesy of the Panhandle-Plains Historical Museum, Canyon, Texas)

her breast, crying emphatically, 'Me Cynthie Ann! Me Cynthie Ann!'

"Her Uncle Isaac took her home with him, riding beside him in his black buggy, a conveyance she had never seen before. For a time Cynthia Ann—Naudah—lived with her sister, Orlena, who had been just a babe in arms the day Cynthia Ann was abducted. But," Mac told Quanah, "your mother felt no kinship with the Anglo relatives who tried to be kind and patient with her."

Mac continued his story. He told Quanah that the family came to understand that his mother, not knowing what had happened to her husband and two sons, was afraid they had been killed somewhere the day she was taken by the Rangers. She mourned their loss Indian fashion, slashing her arms and hacking her hair.

In the next few years, after several efforts to escape the white community, she made half-hearted attempts to relearn white ways. Although she was given a neat bedroom, at first she could not sleep comfortably on the bed and often made a pallet with a quilt and slept on the floor. In the kitchen she did some small tasks. But her heart was not in it.

Then a "white man's disease" took little Prairie Flower's life and, with her loss, the light went out of Cynthia Ann's life. She pined away and died shortly afterward.

Mac finished his story and flipped away the remains of his cigarette. He turned to the stoic young warrior sitting beside him, whose clenched jaws and staring eyes were the only giveaway to the emotions churning inside him. He clapped the young man on the shoulder. "I'm sorry," he said, in Comanche.

Quickly Quanah was on his feet. He didn't know how to say thank you to the white man who had just given him back years he'd missed of his mother's life. But he thrust forward his hand in a gesture he'd seen the white men use, a sign of camaraderie. Mac smiled and clasped the outstretched hand.

Quanah rode away from the treaty council and headed back to his Quahadis band in Texas. He was distressed by what he'd heard of the treaty. But he'd expected as much. Instead of dwelling on that situation, he pondered his mother's life and death. Saddened though he was that she was gone from him forever, it gladdened his heart to have learned that her last days had been spent with a family who loved and cared for her.

CHAPTER 8

Quanah Becomes
a Young Chief

1871

Just as Quanah had suspected, the treaty at Medicine Lodge did nothing to alleviate the conditions of those Indians who had chosen to go and live on the reservations. The chiefs who signed were often unhappy with their decision to live under the white men's supervision. The promised rations were often late arriving, and when they did reach the families, they were not usually to Indian tastes and the clothes seldom fit.

Dismayed after several months of trial, some of the Indians left the reservation, attempting to return to their old ways. Those were immediately sought out by the army, arrested and returned to the reservation, where harsh punishment was meted out.

Quanah rejoined the Quahadis upon his return from the treaty council. One of the few remaining bands who had insisted on remaining free, they still roamed the Staked Plains, inflicting damage on the ever-encroaching Texans wherever they had the opportunity.

They often crossed the Rio Grande and raided into Mexico, returning with large herds to barter among the illicit Comancheros, a mixed group of Mexicans, Apaches and renegade whites. But more and more often they found it difficult to slip past the Mexican army's border guards, as well as the

American army patrols whose forays now arced farther south. For that reason, Chief Bear's Ear decided that on their next raid, they should ride as far as the Pease River, then turn east where many new homesteaders were settling in.

"Our scouts tell us there are many horses to be had," the chief told his men, "and there will be less danger than from the border patrols."

On the appointed day, Quanah rode with them, the little band raiding several small settlements, acquiring a sizable herd of horses, with few pursuers. But by the time they had completed the entire planned route and circled back, the army contingent from Fort Richardson had been alerted to their presence in the area. Fanned out along the lightly wooded hillside, they laid their ambush.

With the horses in an easy trot, the Indians loosely ringed to keep them at a steady pace, they crossed the river, unaware of the ambush. Chief Bear's Ear was one of the first Indians killed. His men, momentarily stunned by the loss of their leader, spent a few hapless moments floundering about in confusion.

Quanah, not knowing what kind of army force was hidden on the tree-lined hill, quickly assessed the Indians' position. Rushing into the breach left by the loss of their chief, he took command. "Turn the horses!" he shouted. "Turn the horses back to the river!"

As Quanah led the drive, one young cavalryman rode down from the hillside and raised his rifle for the kill. In one fluid motion, Quanah swung low over the opposite side of his racing pony, sending a barrage of arrows under his horse's neck. From his concealed position he quickly put his opponent out of action.

Approaching the river, herding the horses before them, Quanah raced through the melee, urging his men to use the herd as a shield, get the horses into the river, then swim them across. The men rallied to his instructions and, although they were fired upon heavily from the opposite shore, no more of the tribe was lost in the encounter.

That evening, safely back in their own camp, the Quahadis mourned the loss of their chief and their friends. The women's death chant filled the night air while the tom-toms carried the story. The combination, a mournful dirge, drifted on the desert breeze.

In the days that followed there were meetings between the older men of the band. A chief had to be elected. The people could not be without a leader. While the elders debated, life went on in the camp. Quanah continued to hunt, alone and with others, providing the people with food. Every day his childhood training, and the lessons learned in adolescence, were put to good use and he was grateful to the grandfathers who had taught him.

No one was more surprised than Quanah, however, when the elders called a council meeting and told him of their appreciation of the way he had handled the encounter with the army. "Because of your wise decisions that day, you saved your brothers' lives. You saved the herd that our lost friends had helped to build. Because of your leadership and bravery," they told him, "we have elected you our new chief."

Quanah was stunned that one so young should have such an honor given to him, but he was pleased to find that his friends, the other young warriors, all agreed with the elders' decision.

Gravely, Quanah accepted the honor and the responsibility. "When I was a young boy," he told his people as they gathered about the tribal campfire to celebrate, "I vowed that when I became a chief, I would fight our enemy, the Texans, until they leave our lands. As your new chief, I pledge to do this!"

With the horses that had been taken in the last raid, the men decided to ride south toward Mexico, to trade with the Comancheros, who provided guns and ammunition in exchange for horses and cattle. They arrived to find that the Comancheros had not been in their usual barter camps lately and decided to press on toward a Mescalero Apache camp instead.

During the day of trading, Quanah's eye fell on the comely

Quanah in front of a tipi. (Courtesy of the Panhandle-Plains Historical Museum, Canyon, Texas)

young daughter of Chief Old Wolf. Quanah watched as she went about her chores and caught her sidelong glance that offered promise. I am ready for a wife, he thought, and children around our tipi.

Bargaining with Old Wolf was not easy. It meant giving up, from his share of the herd, ten of the best horses. But Quanah had decided. He brought the horses to the chief's lodge, and returned to his village with his new bride, Ta-ho-yea.

Although she looked with favor upon her new husband, their marriage was short-lived. Ta-ho-yea was unable to conquer the Comanche language and life was lonely for her. After several months she confided her unhappiness to Quanah. "You have been good to me," she told the young husband, "but I am homesick. Please let me return to my people."

Quanah had noticed her lackluster eyes, so different from those that had sparkled in his direction in the Mescalero camp. She had been a good wife. He would miss her. But he agreed, and sent her with no dishonor back to her people.

Other young women among the Comanches, however, sought the favor of the young chief and, as his prestige grew, according to Comanche custom, he would acquire more than one wife.

CHAPTER 9

The Battle of Blanco Canyon

1871

In 1871, Texas had been a state of the Union for twenty-six years and there still remained a clamor on the frontier for protection against the Indians. The fierce Quahadis, now under the leadership of Quanah, still battled with a vengeance, determined to drive the white men from what they felt were Indian lands, their ancestral home.

The Texas Rangers had been effective through the years, but were hardly a solution, for they rode out only after the "hostiles" had raided and escaped back to their Staked Plains where, so far, white men had not penetrated. By the time the Rangers were assembled, the damage was done, precious time had been lost, and the Indians had disappeared back into their sanctuaries, where they had never been tracked. Small war parties could raid with lightning speed and then disappear beyond the horizon, gone—like a puff of smoke!

Finally, besieged by frantic homesteaders, Indian Agent Lawrie Tatum, formerly devoted to the Quaker peace policy, sent a plea to Washington, D.C., agreeing that stronger measures were necessary to bring all of the remaining free Indians onto reservations.

With glowing recommendations from Gen. Ulysses S. Grant, young Ranald Slidel Mackenzie was selected for the monumental task. During the Civil War, the officer had caught the eye of the general, who had singled him out as "the most promising young officer in the army."

Mackenzie was ordered to assemble the 4th Cavalry at Fort Richardson, Texas, to begin a campaign designed to end the Indian threat once and for all. For himself, and for the army, he declared a vendetta against the Indians, Quanah's "hostile" Quahadis band in particular, taking on his duties with definite ideas of how to locate and terminate the Comanche's most elusive band.

Mackenzie's men soon learned that their grim-visaged young officer was not the ordinary spit-and-polish officer. Quite the opposite. The troops were allowed to appear in uniform with scraggly beards, long hair, and generally unkempt appearance.

Along with this personal freedom, they quickly learned, there would be less time spent reporting for parades around the fort, less time spent polishing brass, less time spent hanging about waiting for orders. All of that time, Mackenzie figured, was better spent in the field.

Along with all of the other changes he instituted, one of his first directives was that the troops should discard the sabers that had long lent such a glamorous flair to their uniforms. "You won't be needing those," he told them emphatically as he began training them in guerilla tactics. They envisioned hand-to-hand combat as he told them he was determined to bring the Indians their own brand of warfare. The force he was assembling, he announced decisively, would be able to fight Indians in any weather, on any terrain.

By August of 1871, the cavalry was ready to take to the field for maneuvers. He marched them from the fort and for nearly a month subjected his troops to the rigors they would encounter in their eventual missions. The men staunchly suffered through the prolonged conditioning in the midst of heat and drought, existing on short food rations and a severely curtailed water supply.

By mid-September, Mackenzie declared his men ready, and

they returned to Fort Richardson for resupplying. The men proudly and mysteriously referred to their time in the field. The ladies were impressed, awed; and the soldiers who had not been included in the newly designed cavalry but had to remain behind to protect the fort were duly envious. After the brief two-day respite, Mackenzie led the men out of the fort again, this time heading west, into Comanche territory, intent upon their mission to range farther into Indian country than any white men had ventured before. Determined to locate Quanah's base of operations at any cost, Mackenzie led his men into the Staked Plains, over buttes, through ravines, in and out of canyons. But there was no sign of Quanah.

Then in early October, the days having turned from summer's blistering heat to a foretaste of what winter would bring, Mackenzie's scouts finally located one of Quanah's camps made up entirely of Quahadis warriors. The scouts raced the miles back to the main company, reporting their findings. Mackenzie was elated.

Halting his men several miles from the area his scouts had pinpointed, he planned his attack for early the next morning. "We will rush the hostiles before sunup," he advised his officers as they gathered in his tent. "Post your guards around the camp," he reminded his aide, Lt. Robert G. Carter, unnecessarily, "and be sure the horses are securely picketed." He himself strode about, checking details before retiring, confident that the next day would bring him victory over his archenemy.

Around midnight, however, it was Quanah who supplied the surprise. He and a few of his braves slipped past Mackenzie's outer guard and stealthily cut loose the tethered horses. Then he directed his young men to race through the camp on horseback, whooping and flapping blankets. The suddenly awakened soldiers experienced shock as the Indians swept right through the center of the camp, stampeding horses ahead of them.

Years later Quanah would chuckle at the memory of that night, his steel-grey eyes softening with mirth as he told the story of capturing seventy fine horses, among them Mackenzie's own prized grey pacer.

The next morning, as Lieutenant Carter checked the outer perimeter posts to assess the night's damage, he spotted a few Indians at a distance, herding army horses. Carter, taking a small band of troopers and the few remaining horses, gave chase. The Indians raced into a ravine with the soldiers thrashing not far behind. The soldiers followed, up one slope and onto a ridge over which the Indians had disappeared. But, just as the cavalrymen reached the summit, they found a large party of Indians waiting for them. Carter realized he had been led into an ambush!

As the waiting Indians galloped full-speed toward them, the troopers fled back down the hillside, hoping to gain the relative safety of the ravine they had just passed through. "The chief," Lieutenant Carter was to report later, "led the bunch on a coal black racing pony, leaning forward on its mane, his heels working nervously in the animal's side, with a six-shooter poised in the air."

One young private yelled to the lieutenant, "My horse is givin' out on me, sir!" and he dropped behind the others. Neither Carter nor any of his men could help the man as the Indians overtook him and brought him down with one shot.

The soldiers were able to gain the ravine and seek the safety of the trees while returning the Indians' fire. The attack on the ravine was broken off shortly, however, when the Indians saw, rapidly approaching, another contingent of troopers racing to the rescue of Lieutenant Carter and his four surviving soldiers.

Retrieving his wounded and dead, Colonel Mackenzie ordered his men back to Fort Richardson to regroup and try again. But for the time, Quanah had clearly won the Battle of Blanco Canyon, and his people remained free.

Later, Carter, describing the ambush, would say that he would never forget the spectacle of the war-painted chief. "His face was smeared with black paint, which gave his features a satanic look!" If Quanah could have been present and heard

Quanah Parker on horseback. (Courtesy of the Panhandle-
Plains Historical Museum, Canyon, Texas)

those words, he would have felt proud that he had accomplished his purpose since the war paint, and the bloodthirsty cries, were intended to intimidate the enemy!

CHAPTER 10

Quanah Shows Compassion

After routing the army at Blanco Canyon, Quanah led his triumphant warriors back to their home camp, deeper yet in the Staked Plains. Spotted by one of his perimeter guards while still miles away, the camp was alerted to their return. Women stopped in their chores, grandfathers woke from late afternoon naps, and children paused in their play. Anxiously the camp waited to see if the homecoming would be a happy one or if their men would return quietly, indicative of lost battles.

It was a murky purple dusk when the exultant braves finally danced their horses into the clearing. Whoops and yells from the warriors clearly spelled out their victory. The camp was jubilant.

Even before the men could alight from their horses, their wives were alongside to take the war gear from them, whether shields and bows and arrows, or pistols and rifles. These the women carried carefully into their lodges and placed in rawhide trunks alongside the walls of the sleeping area. Later the wives would clean and mend the shields. The men would check their bows for tautness, their arrows to be sure they remained line-straight. The pistols and rifles would be cleaned carefully and stored with the remaining ammunition.

The horses' reins were given over then by the men, into the

hands of the older boys, who waited eagerly, jostling for the honor of leading the steeds out to the edge of camp to be hobbled with the rest of the tribe's herd.

Amidst the happy confusion, Lone Oak, exercising his privilege as the band's eldest grandfather, waved his arms and loudly commanded the women, "Quickly, now! Food for our men! A celebration for our brave ones!"

The women scattered, chattering happily as they shared chores. Some gathered brush and heaped it into a high campfire. Others turned their attention to the preparation of food. By nightfall the celebration was underway with the exuberant men dropping cross-legged in a circle around the now blazing fire. Wives and mothers scurried about, offering the men roasted rabbit and squirrel and beef ribs, and bowls of meat scooped from the gravy of cooking pots.

Tom-toms appeared at the outer fringes of the circle, their haunting beat throbbing through the still night air. The drums would set the tone for dancing later, impelling warrior after warrior to spring into spirited circling of the waning fire, moccasined feet pounding in time to the BOOM-BOOM-BOOM, BOOM-BOOM-BOOM, BOOM.

Quanah, meanwhile, had spoken with the village elders. He had received a report on conditions while the younger men had been absent from camp, along with accounts from his scouts. Then he took his accustomed place at the campfire, sitting quietly, presiding proudly, but not taking part in the wild revelry as he might have on other occasions. He ate little, looking on as his men were fed, listening intently, his eyes applauding as each warrior in his turn leaped to his feet and proclaimed his part in the skirmishes that had defeated the Anglo army.

While his eyes glowed with pride, they did not mirror the thoughts that privately troubled him. His people were celebrating one more victory that night, but he knew other battles must surely follow. The Anglo army would regroup and return—again and again. He knew they would be intent upon punishing the Quahadis people who had refused to go onto reservations—to give up their homes, their land—expecting them to forget their heritage and learn to live as the white men.

We must be ready for their return, Quanah thought. But I cannot spoil my people's well-earned celebration with talk of this tonight. Tomorrow, he said to himself, tomorrow the elders must hear my plans.

The next morning, after a troubled sleep, Quanah sent Brown Fox Fur, the camp crier, to gather the elders for a council meeting. The men filed into his lodge, aligning themselves in rows before him as he sat facing them. Quanah passed among them the feathered ceremonial pipe. As they each took two deep puffs and handed the pipe along the line, the younger men of the band quietly entered through the tent flap and sank into rows at the rear of the tipi. Quanah studied the faces of the men who had elected him their young chief. They had supported his views in the past, and now awaited his latest words of wisdom.

Gravely he told them, "I have reports from our scouts, and from our friends who have visited our grandfathers in our absence. While our young men have been away, fighting the Anglo army, the white farmers have continued to move onto our lands."

"Aiee. Aiee," the elders spoke angrily, nodding their heads.

"They till the soil and fence the land. The deer and the buffalo continue to disappear ahead of them."

"Aiee. Aiee," the elders repeated.

"We must fight them just as we fought the Anglo soldiers and drive them from our lands!"

Again assent rose in the throats of the elders. At the rear of the tipi, the young men quietly, delightedly, elbowed each other at the thought of battling the hated, ever-encroaching settlers.

Quanah gestured toward the open tent flap. Beyond it a blazing yellow sun mellowed the day. "The time of Many-Colored-Leaves is upon us," he told them. "With the changing of the leaves, the Comancheros cross their Mexican border to trade with us and our Kiowa and Cheyenne friends. As we ride south to meet the Comancheros, we will raid every farm in our path!"

The old men bobbed their heads up and down and pounded their fists on their knees. "Aiee! Aiee!" From the rear of the tipi came a suddenly unsuppressable echo.

"We will take the farmer's livestock. All of it. He cannot live without them. And we will take his horses. Without them he cannot follow us. He cannot alert his neighbors. Or the army. We will build a herd of hundreds of horses and drive them ahead of us as we move south. We will," he told them, "trade the animals to the Comancheros for guns and ammunition." Pausing for a moment, he continued, heavyhearted, "The Anglo army will return. We must be ready . . . "

The next few days were spent readying the camp for the braves' trip south. They would travel light, carrying with them only what was necessary for the quick hit-and-run raids. Some of the men would take turns herding the growing number of horses as they moved south, while smaller bands would be dispatched to raid the farms; then, with their booty, they would rejoin the larger band.

As usual, their chief rode ahead of his men. They left early in the morning and by noon had reached the first farm that lay in their path. A small farm, Quanah noted, as he raised his right arm, halting his men. He rode closer, staying hidden by the leafy pin oaks, and surveyed the scene more closely.

At the edge of the front porch a sandy yard led to a small vegetable garden. Among the climbing bean vines, a straw-hatted farmer hoed between the rows. On the other side of the yard, in the shade provided by a lone oak tree, his gaunt-faced wife scrubbed clothes in a large tin tub heated by a small fire. Their young son wrestled manfully with a keg of beans freshly picked from the garden, trying to lift it onto the low porch. Just then, the barn door opened and a little girl stepped outside, carefully holding the corners of her calico apron in which she carried eggs she had just collected from under the cackling hens. She had long blond hair falling to her shoulders, as blond as her brothers, lighter than the mother and father's.

Quanah's breath caught at the sight of the child. Was this perhaps the way his mother, Naudah, had looked the day the Indians raided the Anglo fort and took her away? He remembered the words of the interpreter, sitting around Little Belly's campfire that night at the treaty council meeting. Why, I could take this child back to camp! he thought. She could grow into another Naudah!

But no . . . reason overcame his desire. This was no time for taking captives. There were days of hard riding ahead, and days on their return. A captive, especially a girl, would be in their way. The needs of his tribe must come first. He wheeled his horse and returned to his waiting men. "There is little livestock here but we will take what they have. I will go ahead of you and try to send the family into the forest. That will be their line of safety. If they do not fire on us, we will let them live."

His men heard him, with strange feelings. Never before had they seen Quanah offer protection to Anglos. They could not read their young chief's mind, but obeyed unquestioningly his words. They watched as he rode back toward the young family who would see him now for the first time. It was the son who saw him first, riding fast toward them, one palm held high, signing peace.

"Indian!" the boy yelled, abandoning the keg of beans and sprinting across the yard toward his parents.

The man, clutching his hoe as if a weapon, looked where the son was pointing. He saw the war-painted Indian, almost upon them, now slowly pacing his horse up to their yard. The mother reached for the girl, clutching her arm. Eggs spilled from the little girl's apron, cracking unnoticed at her feet. Her blue eyes were wide with wonder. The husband put himself between Quanah and his family.

Relying on the few words of English he had learned during his years of trading with the Comancheros, Quanah said "Go!" pointing to the trees in the dark woods to the rear of the little farm. "Braves come. You go!" After a moment's hesitation, the farmer, knowing he could not reach a weapon to help them, motioned his family to retreat toward the forest behind the house.

Quanah wheeled his horse and with a war whoop, waved his men onto the farm. As their chief had commanded, the Indians drove away the cow that stood just inside the barn and two plowhorses from the corral. The chickens were plucked from their nests with much squawking, their necks broken with quick snaps, their feet quickly bound, before being slung carelessly across the horses' manes. It was a small haul but the Indians did not want to be burdened with plunder on their horse-raiding trip, so the family's cabin was saved.

The farmer and his family cowered in the woods until the Indians were out of sight. Thoroughly mystified at being spared, the young family often repeated the story to other settlers. The spared family did not give up after their encounter and their loss but, helped by families farther east, were able to resupply their lost animals and eke out a living.

Their story astonished many who had come to grips with Quanah and his raiding parties in the years before. But it astonished very few who had similar visits from the bold warrior and his raiders on that particular trip. In comparing stories they found that the young chief had been benevolent to more families along that raiding path. Quanah, who had never been known to torture his captives the way some Indians did, apparently had been swayed by the sight of the little blond girl who reminded him of his mother. And so, some people could remember Quanah later as a chief with a kind heart.

CHAPTER 11

The Attack on Adobe Walls

Embittered by life on the reservation, Comanches from the Kotsoteka band fled and tried to resume their old way of life. Hunted down by the army and charged with breaking the treaty, many of the Indians were killed and more than a hundred captured. The captives were returned to the reservation where they were held as prisoners. The few bands who remained free, fearing the captives would suffer for any further vengeance raids, remained relatively quiet for a time. The Indian agent, taking the quietness to indicate that the Indians had given up fighting for their lands, finally released the prisoners to live once again on the reservation.

With the hostages now free, some of the bands at large resumed attacks on frontier settlements but soon the encroaching settlers became a secondary concern for them.

On the horizon new foes came into focus in the form of greedy hunters and skinners who dealt in buffalo hides. With the updated Sharps long rifles, which insured accurate firepower over a much greater distance, the hunters could kill hundreds of buffalo a day, followed closely by the skinners who took the hides, leaving the carcasses to rot in the sun. The hides, shipped out to the east for commercial tanning, had become a financial enticement to the hundreds of hunters and skinners who streamed onto the Indian lands.

Quanah realized the Indians would go hungry and freeze without the meat of the great beasts for food and the hides for clothing and shelter. So it was with special gladness that Quanah learned the meaning of the victorious cries of a small party of his young braves as they rode into camp one morning, racing their ponies joyfully among the tipis. Quanah emerged from his lodge to greet them.

Little-Boy slid from his pony and stood before the chief. "White hunters!" he exclaimed proudly, pointing to the scalps on the young Indians' lances.

By now most of the camp, alerted to their arrival, gathered to hear the braves' stories. Little-Boy told at length how they had surprised five white hunters who were skinning buffalo they had killed with their long rifles. Gesturing broadly, Little-Boy exclaimed, "They had killed many buffalo. The carcasses were stripped and left to rot. Much food was left to waste—it could have fed many tribes! Wasted!" he spat the word.

Then, with a grin, Little-Boy indicated the five mules his companions had led into camp. Each was heavily ladened with the hides the skinners had already collected. The young braves had tied travois poles onto each side of the mules, making hammocks to drag behind, which were filled with quantities of the buffalo meat they had saved. Quanah clamped a heavy hand on the young brave's shoulder and nodded approval to the young hunters. "Good!" he told them emphatically. "You did well!"

Among those in the crowd listening to Little-Boy's enthusiastic recital, was Esa-tai, the Medicine Man. Later, following Quanah back to his lodge, he told the chief, "I had a dream last night. I saw our men killing many buffalo hunters. Not just five like those killed today, but many times that."

Quanah listened thoughtfully. He and the other chiefs whose people remained free had not joined any large-scale war parties for some time. Fighting the greedy skinners was different. And necessary.

"Just this morning," Esa-tai pressed on, "as I sat on the hill-side waiting to make my prayers at dawn, I had another vision. I saw many white men at a large encampment where buffalo hunters meet. The buildings were not made of wood, as the white settler's homes are, but of adobe."

"That could be the old place called Adobe Walls," Quanah reflected, recalling a small village in the northern part of West Texas. It had once been an old trading post made up of three large buildings roughly strung together, separated from each other by half a hundred yards. The adobe post had years ago fallen into disrepair and disuse, but if Esa-tai's vision was correct, the hunters and skinners could once again be using it as a supply depot.

"If our people make war against the hunters who gather there," Esa-tai assured Quanah, "my medicine will make certain no Indian dies in the attack but all of the whites will! No more hunters and skinners will come. The buffalo will be saved!"

"I will think about it," Quanah replied. The next morning he rode off to confer with chiefs of the Kiowas and Cheyennes. "If the Medicine Man's magic can help us inflict enough damage to close the trading post, our dwindling buffalo herds might be saved," he explained, repeating what Esa-tai had told him.

By the time Quanah returned to his camp several days later, he had the promise of warriors from several tribes to poise an attack on Adobe Walls. Among his own people there was much jubilation, singing, and dancing around the campfire that night.

Esa-tai was not to take part in the battle, but was to ride his yellow-painted horse to a vantage point from which he could watch the battle and direct his magic.

Quanah led the main war party to within sight of the village, arriving after midnight. The Indians waited in silence, ready to strike just before dawn, when, Esa-tai had said, they could surprise the sleeping hunters. Quanah studied the layout of the village with its two mercantile stores, saloon and small restaurant where one of the men's wives cooked for the itinerant hunters. Carefully the chief reviewed his plan of attack.

Unknown to Quanah and his war party, however, the element of surprise would not prevail. In the early morning hours a sharp crack awakened the owner of the saloon who rushed to the hunters for help, telling them that the center pole holding the earthen ceiling of his saloon had cracked. The ceiling was in danger of collapse. The men tumbled from their beds and repaired the threatened structure.

By then, fully awake, and with dawn so near, the twenty-eight men decided not to return to bed but to prepare instead for the day's work. It was Billy Dixon who spotted some of the Indians as he walked out to hitch up his wagon. Racing back to the safety of the adobe saloon, he sounded the alarm just ahead of the Indians' strike, their element of surprise lost.

With Esa-tai's promise of immunity from the white men's bullets, the Indians charged recklessly up to the buildings. Hunters firing from the small slit-windows, with the extra protection offered by the thick adobe walls, were able to withstand the onslaught, badly outnumbered as they were. It was the Sharps rifles, with which they slaughtered the buffalo, far superior to anything the Indians possessed, that made the final difference in the outcome of the battle. The Sharps fired faster and farther. No amount of Indian bravado or daring could offset the superior firepower.

More than once that day, Quanah's mind returned to Esa-tai's vision of total victory and no Indian deaths. By day's end, surveying the battleground, he counted fifteen fallen warriors.

After a long, unsuccessful siege, Quanah deliberated with the other chiefs. They decided the long rifles were more than a match for their own and chose to retire from the field of battle.

Angrily, some of the Indians turned on the Medicine Man, berating him for his not-so-magic medicine. Esa-tai, in turn, claimed that one of the Indians, on the way to battle, must have killed a skunk, thus spoiling his magic. Quanah also, was bitter about the outcome of the battle but felt that Esa-tai had suffered enough in humiliation and would condone no further punishment.

Thus Quanah, suffering his first setback as chief, in a battle, led his dejected warriors back home to the Staked Plains. It was not just a lost battle, he knew, but a lost cause. Now it was only a matter of time before his people would more drastically feel the loss of the great herds he had tried to protect from annihilation.

CHAPTER 12

The Fateful Battle
of Palo Duro Canyon

1875

The attack on Adobe Walls, although it was a failure for the Indians, brought an order from Washington, D.C., that a concentrated effort must be made to locate and punish the culprits. Consequently, it fell to Colonel Mackenzie to attempt, once again, to provide a plan that would once and for all flush the Quahadis from their desert lair.

After much deliberation, a coordinated push was decided upon, with Maj. William Price moving eastward from Fort Union; Lt. Col. J.W. Davidson converging from Fort Sill; and Col. G.P. Buell approaching from the Red River vicinity. Colonel Mackenzie with his troops would come up from his base camp near the Fresh Water Fork of the Brazos. The four-pronged pincer movement, Washington hoped, would surely squeeze the remaining free Indians from their hideouts in the Staked Plains.

From early in the fall until midwinter, the cavalry units attempted to tighten a noose around the Indians in their perimeter where Quanah's band, along with a few other Comanche, Kiowa and Cheyenne bands was known to be holding out. They were, as yet, content with the knowledge that no white man had ever found their Palo Duro Canyon hideout.

But they had not figured on the inevitable. Under duress, a

captured Comanchero gave Mackenzie's men detailed instructions for reaching the canyon. He diagrammed the front
entrance, which, if blocked by troopers descending the slender trail one at a time, would not allow room for the Indians to
elude their captors. Nor could they escape on horseback
through the rear as the canyon walls were too steep.

In the predawn hours, Mackenzie led his men to the canyon
trail. Below were camps of the holdout Kiowas, Comanches,
and Cheyennes. The troopers, on foot, descended, stealthily
inching single-file down the steep incline that took them from
the rim of the canyon to its floor far below. The Indians, caught
off guard by overconfidence, their hideaway never before
having been penetrated, awoke to find the first of a burgeoning
army force which had crept in among them, while the balance
of Mackenzie's command quickly negotiated, one by one, the
steep entranceway.

As usual, the warriors shunted their women and children to
the rear, giving them a head start toward escape while the men
fought a delaying action. The Indians retreated from their
camp, backing from tipi to tipi. Firing from behind boulders
and trees as they withdrew, they scattered in the darkness,
seeking the lofty walls at the far end of the vast canyon.

As dawn turned to daylight, the army could see that the
surviving Indians had been able to clamber up the canyon walls
and escape but had left many of their dead behind them. Even
more important to Mackenzie was the fact that, as a result of
the surprise attack, the Indians had to flee with only the clothes
on their backs. Pleased with that turn of events, the colonel
rode through the canyon with a satisfied smile as he surveyed
the all-important, life-sustaining ingredients the Indians had
left behind. Their tipis, their clothes, their winter food supplies.
He smiled broadly when his adjutant reported, "They had to
flee on foot, sir! They must have left a thousand horses
throughout the canyon! The men are rounding them up now.
That's a lot of horses to drive back to camp."

With a grim smile, Mackenzie ordered, "Burn everything!

Put it all to the torch. The lodges, the clothing left behind, the winter foodstuff. Everything! When they return to pick up the pieces, they'll find nothing."

"Those who escaped won't last long," he predicted. "Afoot, with no provisions, they'll starve or freeze before long."

He watched the thick smoke spiraling up toward the sky, then turned once again to his adjutant. "Now have the men round up the horses the Indians left behind and shoot them."

Stunned, his aide looked at him with disbelief. "Shoot them, sir?"

"Shoot them!" Mackenzie repeated sternly. "Kill every last one of them. I want those who escaped to see them dead—to know they have no recourse but to come onto the reservation if they want to survive."

The soldiers could understand his logic, but to cavalrymen, to whom horses were an integral part of their lives, it was difficult to believe they were being asked to destroy good mounts. Mackenzie, too, was "cavalry," but he was adamant in his command, and watched as the animals were destroyed.

By a quirk of fate, Quanah's band had not been in the canyon that night. He learned of the fate of the others later as survivors straggled into his camp miles away, half-frozen and hungry. He saw that they were fed and clothed, his little band sharing what they had.

In the days that followed, one chief after another stopped by his camp for a conference over the campfire. Sharing a pipe, they remarked sadly, "I am taking my people to the army post to surrender. There are too few of us and too many of the Anglos. We must give up our lands, our way of life, if our people are to survive."

Quanah watched them go, knowing that his people now stood alone in the fight against the Anglos. He admitted to himself that with the loss of the buffalo, and the army now tracking only his small band, their fate was sealed. It was only a matter of time . . .

CHAPTER 13

Surrender at Fort Sill

A year later, Quanah could no longer ignore the fact that defeat was inevitable.

If he had been alone, faced by an enemy, he would have chosen the death of a warrior in mortal combat. But he was a chief with a starving band. Each day he watched them grow weaker though the men ranged farther and farther afield, searching for food. They returned, more often than not, empty-handed, with stories of whole herds of buffalo slaughtered by the greedy hunters, the stripped carcasses left to rot, bones bleaching on the windswept plains. Their former hunting grounds were reduced to mile upon mile of stench-filled prairie, the skies black with circling buzzards.

After much deliberation, Quanah called a meeting of all of the men of his band. As they sat about the fire in his lodge, he explained that he felt that surrender was the only answer if the Quahadis were to survive.

"I promise you, brothers and fathers and sons, that I will always remain your chief, your liaison between the Anglos and our band. I only ask," he said to them, "that while you walk the white man's path for the sake of peace, you will always remember your Comanche heritage with pride!"

For the last time he watched the women prepare to move

camp. Down came the meat-drying racks and the buffalo-hide tipis. Travois were strapped to the pack animals. There was the usual bustle of moving day but none of the accustomed happy camaraderie as the heavy jobs were shared, none of the excitement of looking forward to the next campsite and the possibility of seeing old friends from other tribes again. Even the children, usually boisterous, bursting with anticipation, had caught the saddened mood of the adults and, subdued, kept to the fringes of the preparations.

Heavyhearted, Quanah sent word to Fort Sill that he was bringing his people in to the reservation. His decision was received at the fort with jubilation in most quarters. The "scourge of the plains," from his days as a young warrior to his days as a chief, was putting an end to warfare on the frontier!

His old adversary, Colonel Mackenzie, however, could not fully savor the news. He welcomed the peace it would bring, but he could not in all honesty know the feeling of personal triumph he would have liked, as a soldier who has won a hard, arduous battle. He realized that he had been instrumental in Quanah's downfall, but it was neither he nor his U.S. Army troops who, in the end, had finally defeated Quanah. It was "circumstances," he knew. It was impending starvation, annihilation, brought on by white men's greed.

So he watched with mixed emotions that second day of June 1875, when the chief rode stoically into Fort Sill, at the head of his shrunken band of Quahadis, the last great chief to surrender. As he stood on the porch of his Bachelor Officers' Quarters, Mackenzie hoped Quanah could see that he stood at attention, one brave leader acknowledging another.

Quanah rode, erect, eyes forward, toward the tall flag pole he had been told would be the surrender site. From the line of soldiers on his right, a sergeant rode up beside him and reached for Quanah's reins. With a slight movement, Quanah turned his horse's head away and in pidgin English told the sergeant "No! No lead me like cow!"

Years later, when Quanah's English was better, in a candid

interview, with pardonable pride he put the record straight as to how he came onto the reservation: "I came to Fort Sill. No ride me in like a horse or lead me by halter like a cow. Me had big war. I fought . . . Mackenzie. He brave man, good soldier, but uses 2,000 men, many wagons, horses, mules. Me. I had 450 braves, no supply train, ammunition and guns like him. Mackenzie," he said emphatically, "no *catch* me!"

The government gave Quanah a white man's house on the reservation. He had only known tipis before, buffalo-skin lodges. Pallets of soft animal skins for sleeping, campfires with cooking pots for eating. Now there would be wooden houses of the white man, beds for sleeping. Tables for eating. So much to learn . . .

And, he realized, his people would have much to learn, too, in order to survive in this new world. He had a double responsibility now. Not only must he adapt, but he must also set an example for his people to follow. First, he explained to his wives (Comanche custom dictated that a man could have as many wives as he could support) that their older children must be enrolled in a school "many moons away," where they would learn the white man's language and the white man's ways.

Before they left, he gathered his young sons to his side and said, "Do you remember when you were first learning to hunt buffalo? You were taught to think like the buffalo as you approached the herd downwind; to think which way he would dodge to outrun a brave closing in for the kill; to think of running at the center of the herd where he could not be cut out of the bunch and made vulnerable. To think," he reminded them, "like a bear when he is paced by a tracker. To think like a deer as it leaps into the foliage to elude a hunter. Learn to think, now," he finished simply, "like the white man. It is the only way to survive."

Quanah Parker in a three-piece suit and derby hat.
(Smithsonian Institution Photo No. 50322)

CHAPTER 14

Quanah Named Chief of All Comanches

Although the Comanches were made up of many loosely knit bands, each having its own chief, the governmental agencies felt that having one chief over all, on the reservation, would result in a tighter rein on problems. Knowing Quanah's leadership was respected by the Indian community, they quickly designated him to that post, feeling certain the move would be ratified by the Indian Council.

The first few days of his new life were very difficult for the young chief. Not only did he have to walk a narrow line between the red and white communities, hoping to engineer an enduring peace, but he, too, was learning a completely different way of life.

Quanah presented a striking picture, striding about Fort Sill's reservation, meeting with the Indian agent, then with his own people. He stood arrow-straight, taller than average for an Indian, his skin deeply bronzed, his black hair parted in the center and drawn back in two braids. His slate-grey eyes were the only feature marking his white heritage. Soon he began to moderate his appearance, sometimes sporting a three-piece suit with a white shirt and colorful tie, leather shoes, and a black derby hat.

Quanah, nearly thirty years old, came onto the reservation

knowing only enough pidgin English to allow him to trade with
the occasional white men he had encountered through the
Comancheros, with whom he had traded for horses and guns
as well as cloth, beads and cooking utensils his wives had
wanted. Now, on the reservation, with the aid of a government-
appointed tutor, he began haltingly to master the speech of
his mother's people.

He was also given a small office in the Indian agency building and was able to watch officials come and go about their
business. After a few weeks, when he was more comfortable in
his new setting, he entertained other chiefs with tongue-in-
cheek descriptions of his new job as chief over all. Displaying
his wry sense of humor, he showed them how he sat at his new
desk with his chair tilted back and his feet propped up on the
desk, smoking a "seegar" and reading a newspaper, "like white
man," he told them. "Soon white man come in, sit down at my
desk and say, 'Quanah, I need talk to you.' I turn in my chair,
blow seegar smoke in his face and say, 'What can I do for you?'"

In the days to follow, just as he affected changes in himself,
he also initiated changes in the lives of his people, and just as
adamantly opposed any unfavorable ones for them. Using his
newfound position, Quanah promoted as much independence
as possible for the Indians while protecting their interests.

One day, for instance, he learned with dismay that army
recruiters were circulating among young Comanche braves
attempting to sign them up for an all-Indian cavalry unit. He
quickly stepped in, refusing to let the young men join. "It would
be a good experience for these young Indians," the recruiters
tried to tell him.

Quanah remained adamant, reminding them, "The white
men sent missionaries among my people here on the reservation preaching that war is wrong. Now you try to lure our young
men into your army. It cannot be!" he said.

On the other hand, he gave wholehearted approval to the
idea of a Comanche police force on the reservation. He realized how difficult it must be for the tribal elders to accept young

white men telling them what to do. It would be better, he reasoned, for his people to police themselves rather than have the white men do it. It might take a while, he knew, but he started planning for that future move.

CHAPTER 15

Quanah Visits
His Mother's People

From the time of his mother's disappearance after the Battle of Pease River while Quanah was still a young brave, he often dreamed of seeing her again. At the Medicine Lodge Treaty Council, however, when he was in his early twenties, he had learned from Mac, the interpreter, that she had died in Texas six or seven years earlier.

After he moved onto the reservation he seriously considered trying to locate his mother's grave—possibly even meeting her family. Hesitantly Quanah approached the Indian agent with the idea and asked permission to leave the reservation for a trip to Texas.

The sympathetic agent, reviewing in his mind Quanah's consistently good work and untiring attempts toward bettering relations between the Indian and white communities, agreed to help in his quest. He instructed Quanah in how to advertise in the newspaper for information regarding Cynthia Ann Parker's family with respect to locating his mother's grave.

After what seemed to Quanah an eternity, there was a reply from a gentleman living just south of Fort Worth. He wrote that he had learned of Quanah's search and said he would direct him to her grave. The letter was signed as a "cousin."

Sharing in Quanah's excitement, the agent secured for him

a rough map of the area through which he would be traveling. He also gave him a short letter explaining that Quanah was the son of Cynthia Ann Parker and was going to visit her people in Texas. He asked that people help him along the way, where they could.

Quanah left Fort Sill astride one of the horses from his herd. In his pocket he carried the map and the letter of introduction.

By then, almost everyone in Texas knew the story of Cynthia Ann's abduction by the Indians and many had also learned of the excellent reputation her Comanche son had gained, after his surrender, as a liaison between the red and white people. Since he was the son of Cynthia Ann Parker, many were inclined to forgive his past in the light of his half-white ancestry. On several occasions, however, Quanah was turned away from homesteads where he sought directions, or grain for his horse. More than one irate farmer ordered him off his property at rifle point with harsh denouncements.

One elderly gentleman Quanah encountered, however, read his letter and was so touched by the circumstances he thoughtfully aided Quanah by adding more details to the map he carried, marking creeks and roads and drawing other helpful landmarks. This information soon led Quanah to the front gate of the cousin who had written to him and who proved to be as friendly as his letter had sounded.

As he had promised, he guided Quanah out to the little cemetery. To reach it, they had to pass through a cattle pasture and thence through a cow lot. The grave, being remote, had not seen care in several years, it seemed, and the neglect saddened Quanah.

During Quanah's short stay, the newfound cousin filled in a few more details of Cynthia Ann's return to Texas. Following the death of her daughter, Prairie Flower, he said, she was so depressed the family thought a change of scenery might be good for her and she was sent to stay with her younger sister, Orlena (who had been that babe in arms when Cynthia Ann was captured). Although Orlena and her husband made her welcome in their home and her sister tried to ease her back into family ways, nothing lessened Cynthia Ann's desire to return to her Indian family. She still, at that point, did not know if her husband, Peta Nocona, and her young sons were alive.

Orlena promised Cynthia Ann that at the end of the Civil War, which was now raging between the North and South, she would find a way to return her to the Comanches. A virulent influenza epidemic, however, felled Cynthia Ann. Already weakened by heartbreak, she soon succumbed to the flu.

When Quanah's cousin had told him as much family history as he could, he directed him along to the home of Cynthia Ann's younger brother, Silas (who also had been present at her abduction), and his wife, Janey. "Uncle Silas" greeted Quanah warmly and welcomed him into his house. Janey sat him down to a hot meal in the kitchen, and then, knowing he must be tired from his long journey, showed him to a small neat bedroom. "Your mother slept here when she was with us," Janey told him.

She turned back the coverlet and quilt, fluffed up the featherpillow, and, setting a lamp on the lace doily-covered dresser, left him alone with his thoughts.

Quanah spent most of that summer with Silas and Janey. Having studied the white man's language on the reservation he was better able to converse and felt quite comfortable speaking his halting English with his mother's family.

Going out each morning with his uncle, following as Silas went through his chores, Quanah learned something of farming and farm life. He saw firsthand the milking of the cows, watched the pigs being "slopped," and witnessed for the first time the picking of cotton. Although Quanah was certain he never wanted to change from ranching to farming, he was eager to learn each new operation of the farm. In the kitchen, where he sometimes sat and drank coffee and talked while she worked, Janey introduced him to breadmaking, pickling, and the churning of butter.

Often, in the evening, the two men would sit out on the

long, low front porch and smoke while Janey finished her kitchen chores. In those "quiet times" Silas tried to introduce Quanah to more information about his mother's family.

"Your mother's brother, John," he told him one evening, "was abducted at the same time as Cynthia Ann was. He was only six years old at the time. Seems he was bartered away to another tribe, the first night out, and he never saw his sister again. He learned Comanche ways and fit into the Indians' life, and they eventually adopted the little towhead into the tribe. When he was grown, he went with the men on a raid into Mexico and on the way back he was stricken with the dread smallpox disease. The Indians had seen smallpox before, and knew how it could wipe out whole tribes. Fearful of that, they left him out in the desert to die. A young Mexican girl, a captive from the raid, stayed behind with him and nursed him through the illness. He returned to Mexico with her, married her and settled down near the border to become a rancher."

"I would like to get to know this John Parker," Quanah said, and so Silas made the necessary arrangements.

It was early autumn when Quanah once again saddled up, a new map and letter of introduction in hand, for the long ride south toward the Mexican border. He found John Parker's hacienda where he lived with his wife, Juanita. John was as fascinated by Quanah's story as Quanah was by John's and they became fast friends. Quanah learned how John had fought in the Civil War until wounded, and how he had returned to Texas and had been reunited with his family, and now was living the life of a hardworking rancher.

Much time had passed since Quanah began his quest for his mother's family, and he decided to start back to the reservation before the winter months set in. With a happier heart he said goodbye, thankful for the months he had spent getting to know his mother's family.

Back on the reservation, once more among his own people, Quanah was anxious to impart the wonders he had seen in his travels, and spoke of the many nice, kind white people he had met. One of the older Indian men listening to his account, still considering Texans his enemy, was plainly disturbed to hear Quanah speak of them in such glowing terms.

"If you like the white Texans so much, why didn't you stay there!" he challenged.

In his heart, Quanah understood the man's bitterness. Hadn't he, himself, felt the same animosity to the Texans until he had an opportunity to meet them, to see the other side? He looked at the men of his tribe gathered about him, waiting for his reply. With his humor surfacing once more, he said to his challenger with a smile, "Down there I'm just a plain Indian— here I'm a great chief!"

CHAPTER 16

Quanah Is Appointed Judge

The Comanches on the reservation at Fort Sill made it known that, just as they preferred to police themselves, they also preferred their own brand of justice. Eventually three Indian judges were appointed, with Quanah as one of those named to the bench, a position he would hold for a decade.

Quanah sat with the other two judges twice a month at which time minor tribal offenses were brought before them. In dispensing justice, any offenses were looked at from the Indian point of view. Indiscretions were seen as having been committed against the person, rather than against society as a whole, as in the white men's concept.

There were few cases of theft to contend with for, if an Indian desired something that belonged to a neighbor, all that was necessary was a request or a gentle hint and the object was usually freely given, as a friendly gesture.

More often than not, the cases that came up before the court were those concerning a straying wife. In the olden days such an indiscretion would have arbitrarily resulted in such dire consequences as the wife having the tip of her nose cut off! (And that usually was done by the wronged husband, who did not wait for tribal law consent.) Thus the wayward wife not only suffered pain, but also the humiliation of being branded an adulteress by all concerned. The more usual practice became, however, through the new judicial system for the husband to demand compensation from the other man in the form of a liberal payment of horses, thereby increasing the husband's wealth.

The more serious cases, such as, infrequently, murder, were subject to a higher court which convened in Wichita Falls, Texas.

As Quanah's years on the reservation progressed, he learned much from friends he made among the rich white cattlemen about the white men's ways in the field of finance and development. He gained more power and prestige and became a shrewd hand at negotiating deals that would enhance his people's holdings.

Just such a deal came to mind one day as Quanah was riding his favorite black stallion out, overseeing his own property as he often did. He rode on, to the far reaches of the reservation, reminiscing about how the buffalo herds had once dominated the landscape. Now, on the range, just beyond the reservation, there were instead, great herds of longhorn cattle owned by wealthy ranchers. To get those cattle to the eastern markets, the ranchers had to mount long, hard cattle drives. They had to plan many extra days on the trail, skirting Indian lands, in order to reach the Kansas rail lines. Quanah suddenly had the glimmering of an idea. Hastily he rode back to the fort and rushed into the Indian agent's office.

"If the ranchers were allowed to cross Indian lands with their herds," he reasoned, "they could cut days off the drive. They could pay their cowboys less for the drive and the cattle would get to the market faster and fatter . . . for a fee," he added, "of, say, a dollar a head. Paid to the Indian community."

The agent smiled at Quanah's shrewd assessment of the situation and agreed to speak to the ranchers while Quanah made the same proposal to his people. Both sides saw a considerable gain to be made and an agreement was soon drawn up between them, with Quanah's Comanches receiving handsome dividends.

Later, using the same power of deduction, Quanah was able to phase in another financially successful idea. He arranged to lease grazing rights on Indian lands to the three wealthiest Texas cattlemen of that day: Dan Waggoner, Charles Goodnight and Burk Burnett.

Even more compelling problems were placed on Quanah's shoulders—some of which he could not solve for his people's betterment. The treaty that so many Comanche bands had signed at Medicine Lodge Council, providing them with homes, food and clothing for thirty years, had come to a close. Quanah tried to gain a little more time for the people covered by the treaty which his own band had not signed. He traveled to Washington, D.C., to beg for a five-year extension. "Some of my people," he told President McKinley, "are not yet ready to fend for themselves against greedy white men who try to cheat them." But the president was adamant in backing the congressional proposal and the Indian lands were split; the treaty became history. Quanah had to return home and repeat to his people what he had been told. "It has to be," he said sadly.

In one regard, however, Quanah turned a deaf ear to the white man's rules. According to Indian custom, a man could have as many wives as he could afford. Over the years Quanah had become quite affluent and had acquired seven wives (not counting his first whom he had returned to her Apache people when she could not adjust to Comanche life). His first wife Weckeah, bore him five children; Chony bore three; Mahcheetowooky had two; Aerwuthtakeum had two; Coby had one son; Topay had four, two of whom died in infancy; and Tonarcy, his latest wife, had none.

Burk Burnett decided Quanah and his burgeoning family should have more adequate quarters and proposed to have a house built for them, himself. He told Quanah to pick the place he'd like to have the new home. Shortly afterward there arrived a train of wagons bringing in the lumber. The house was to

Quanah and his wife on the porch of his home, which was known locally as the "Comanche White House." (Courtesy of the Panhandle-Plains Historical Museum, Canyon, Texas)

have twelve rooms, enough to accommodate each wife and her children, with additional rooms for all to socialize as "family." Large and square, with a porch that stretched around three sides on the lower level and a balcony upstairs, the house became known locally as the "Comanche White House." It did, indeed, see many of Washington's top officials as guests, including "Teddy" Roosevelt when he became President of the United States. At Quanah's request, twenty-two large white stars were painted on the roof!

But the fact that Quanah could afford so many wives, and provide adequate housing for them and their children, did not deter the white community from being very vocal in their disapproval of the plural marriages. Several times the Indian agent spoke to Quanah about his many wives but each time Quanah pointedly ignored his remarks. Finally, at the commissioner's insistence, the agent sought out Quanah again and cornered him for a showdown.

"You simply must," he told the chief, "decide on which one wife you want to keep and tell the others they must leave your house."

Solemnly Quanah considered the ultimatum, bewildered by the perplexing task assigned him. Finally, shaking his head, he turned to the official with the challenge, "YOU TELL 'UM WHICH ONE!"

The official, for the first time viewing the dilemma from the standpoint of the husband unwilling to face so many infuriated wives, was stymied and gave up!

CHAPTER 17

Quanah Helps Young Anglos

Quanah had finished his breakfast later than usual and was lingering over a second cup of coffee with his wife, Tonarcy, who enjoyed extra-sweetened coffee almost as much as Quanah did. He was deep in thought as he moved away from the table in the kitchen of the Big House, which Burk Burnett had built for him years ago, and walked out onto the wraparound front porch, cup in hand. A pale yellow sun spread a leaden cast over the midmorning sky. Quanah eyed it reflectively, remarking over his shoulder to his wife, "We could get a storm before the day is over."

She nodded in silent agreement, the ominous sky reminding her of some of the storms they had endured throughout the years on the broad expanse of the Staked Plains. In those days their tipis had borne the brunt of the wind and rain and hail. Now with the great wooden house to shelter them, Tonarcy was no less intimidated by the fierce storms that often swept across their lands.

Squinting into the distance, Quanah watched low red clouds of dust rising on the horizon indicating intense activity in that area of his ranch spread. "Buffalo Cliff's got 'em out there branding today," he told Tonarcy. "I'd better get along and see how it's going."

97

"Buffalo Cliff can't handle it without you?" Tonarcy chided her husband gently. He had just returned a week earlier from a long tiring trip to Washington, D.C., where he had met with the president in an unsuccessful bid for an extension on his people's land treaty. Tonarcy worried that he needed rest. She had often tried to entice him to let his foreman carry more of the burden of the ranch but Quanah could not break from old ways. Every morning he rode out about his acres, overseeing the daily chores.

"Buffalo Cliff can handle it—yes!" Quanah retorted. "But he's working with some new young hands we took on last week for the branding and I want to see how well they are working out."

Tonarcy took his empty cup and started back to the kitchen. As he stepped off the low front porch onto the dusty yard, she called after him apprehensively, "Try to get back before the storm hits."

Quanah strode off toward the corral where he cut out a big red roan and saddled it. Turning the horse out of the gate he hit a gallop toward the dust cloud ahead. As he rode, his mind went back to the evening before when he had been sitting on his front porch, his chair tilted back against the wall, watching the approach of dusk.

In the distance he spotted a lone rider coming along the thread of trail leading to the house from the main road nearly a mile away. He watched the rider swaying gently in the saddle, riding easy, a little wearily, as if he had covered quite a few miles. As he drew closer, Quanah could see it was no one he knew and surmised it was another drifter looking for a job.

As the horseman drew closer, passing through the front gate, he hesitated, looking at the Big House, then took note of the barn area and the corral. He turned his horse in that direction where several ranch hands were sitting along the fence, talking over a last smoke.

Quanah watched as the young man asked for the foreman and Buffalo Cliff's bunkhouse was pointed out to him. The cowboy entered the building, came out very shortly after, mounted his horse and started back toward the main gate. Quanah rose from his chair and beckoned to him. "Looking for work?"

"Yes sir." The young man halted, then turned his horse toward Quanah who approached with a friendly hand out. "This is my place. Name's Quanah Parker."

The cowboy slipped off his horse and strode forward, whipping off his dusty hat. The hair beneath it was almost as dusty as the hat itself. "Marvin," he said, fishing a red plaid kerchief from a back pocket and rubbing at his sweaty face. "Billy Marvin."

"Where'd you come from?" Quanah wanted to know.

"Just up from Stoddard's spread. A day's ride south. I was there for three months till a hand came back from taking some cattle to market. They didn't need me no more. I been hittin' all the ranches along, but seems too late in the season. Ever'body's all filled up."

"Know anything about branding?" Quanah asked.

"Used to help my pa, back in Texas." The young man hung his head a moment. "Times got bad for my pa and ma during the war and we lost the farm. They died a while back. I been on the road since, lookin' for steady work."

"Wait a minute," Quanah told him. "Maybe we could just use one more hand around here."

He walked out to the foreman's cabin and confronted Buffalo Cliff. "Think you could find something for this kid to do around here?" Quanah asked. "He's got no family—and doesn't appear to me to be just a regular drifter."

"If you say so, boss. Boy, you just can't turn away anybody, can you?" Buffalo Cliff said in mock exasperation.

"He's got no family," Quanah repeated. "You'll try him out?"

"I'll put him on the payroll," Buffalo Cliff said as he had done so many times in the past when Quanah had gone to bat for a struggling, hungry young cowboy.

Quanah took the news back to the grateful young man and

told him, "Go around to the kitchen. You missed supper but the cook'll find you something."

Quanah's memory of the night before was interrupted as he approached the bunch of sweating, swearing cowhands, actively engaged in branding some of Quanah's newly acquired herd. Buffalo Cliff, who had been watching Quanah's approach, peeled his horse away from the activity to meet him.

"How's it going?" Quanah asked .

"Good, so far. On schedule." Most of the young men were Indian hands who had worked for Quanah for a year or so, some he had acquired through the Indian agency on the post. There were a few worthless drifters among the Anglos, and Quanah knew that, true to form, they would hang around a few days, a few weeks, and, bored, would move on after payday.

Then he spotted the young man who had ridden in the night before. The boy, his young muscles straining, caught a calf with a short rope, threw the struggling animal on its side, and held it fast for the branding iron. "How's that one working out?" Quanah asked.

"Seems like you picked a good worker there, boss. He was the first one out of the bunkhouse this morning. The first one saddled after breakfast. And he hasn't loafed off yet."

Satisfied, Quanah turned back toward the house, calling back to Buffalo Cliff, "Try to get in before the storm."

With unspoken admiration, the foreman watched as Quanah rode away, back toward the Big House. He'd been Quanah's foreman for many years, and knew him well. He realized that Quanah's exposure to his mother's family during his visit with them in Texas had colored his feelings during his following years on the reservation. A certainty seemed to have formed in his mind that there were good Anglos among the Texans and he no longer condemned them all for the fact that he was now reduced to reservation living rather than being the free-spirited Comanche he once had been. Just as he tried to help his own people, he now extended a hand to hardworking young Texans who came to his ranch looking for work. Buffalo Cliff had seen it happen before. Quanah felt sorry for homeless young hands, and not only hired them—but often offered to adopt them!

CHAPTER 18

Quanah's Narrow Escape and New Discovery

As Quanah's role on the reservation expanded, so did his circle of friends and his experiences. At the urging of his friends, the wealthy cattlemen Dan Waggoner and Burk Burnett, he began attending the annual livestock show in Fort Worth, Texas. And several times he was called upon to make trips to the capitol in Washington, D.C., to lobby for Indian rights. He became familiar with the "Iron Horse," as he had once upon a time called the train, riding it several times between Oklahoma and the U.S. capital.

Once while planning a trip to Washington, realizing he enjoyed traveling, he announced he would like to visit the Carlisle Indian School in Pennsylvania. Several of his children had attended school there and he had one in attendance at the time. He decided to take Tonarcy along.

Newspapers took pleasure in reporting that the chief and his wife both appeared in Washington and at the school, fashionably dressed. In Washington, Tonarcy wore a satin dress, and at the school she arrived in a Basque jacket and skirt of gaily colored material, wearing high heels, while Quanah appeared in a three-piece business suit, sporting a gold watch chain across his vest.

In the school's auditorium one evening they were entertained by a band and choir. Afterwards, when Quanah was introduced, he made a short speech saying he had come 2,000 miles to see the school and his child and that he found "everything good."

His trips to Fort Worth increased, not only to attend the livestock show, but also frequently to represent Comanche interests in which he dealt with the ranchowners. One of those trips was memorable.

He had arrived in Fort Worth accompanied by another Indian named Yellow Bear. They registered at the city's finest hotel and then met the foreman of the Waggoner ranch for dinner. Afterward, Yellow Bear said he was tired and returned to the hotel. A few hours later, Quanah returned, and finding Yellow Bear asleep, undressed, turned out the gas light and went to bed, too. However, he failed to turn the gas valve off completely. Throughout the night a small amount of gas continued to flow into the room.

It was not until sometime the next day that the hotel management was alerted to the smell of escaping gas on that floor. By then both Quanah and Yellow Bear were unconscious. Quanah had been sleeping near a partially opened window, however, and though dangerously ill, survived, but Yellow Bear could not be revived.

With that sad occurrence to haunt him each time he had to return to Fort Worth, he made his visits less often. It was during one of those trips, as he stood by the corral studying the cattle in the pen, that a man beside him asked if he was Quanah Parker.

"Well, I declare," the man said. "I saw a picture of your mother once," he observed.

"A picture of my mother!" Quanah was incredulous. "Where?"

The man scratched his head and tried to recall. "Can't rightly remember what town it was in. But it was in a photographer's studio window. Picture of her and her baby."

Quanah quickly sought out Burk Burnett and repeated the conversation, asking, "How can I see this picture?"

Burk walked his friend to the newspaper office and showed Quanah how to advertise for anyone with knowledge of the picture of Cynthia Ann to please contact him. Then, just as Quanah had waited for a reply from his mother's relatives so he could make the trip to Texas, now he waited just as anxiously, hoping someone would see the ad who might know where his mother's picture could be found.

It was several weeks before a reply came. The Indian agent called to say, "Quanah, I have a package for you." It had come in the mail with a letter from Sul Ross, the very captain who had led the Texas Rangers' attack on the camp at Pease River, the day Naudah was taken captive.

Quanah took the package in nervous fingers and hurried into his little office to open it. Fumbling the strings aside. Quanah ripped open the wrapping paper, and there it was—a picture of his mother with little Prairie Flower at her breast! Naudah looked back at Quanah with the same sweet face he remembered, but in the picture her hair was cut shorter than when he had last seen her—cut as if in mourning—and she was dressed in the calico of white women.

Quanah stared at the picture for a long while with a lump in his throat. Not only did he have a picture of his mother, but he had just witnessed another instance proving that not all Texans were as cruel as he once believed. Sul Ross, in his kind gesture, was just such proof. Sul Ross, the man who had taken his mother from him, from her Comanche family, had seen his plea for her picture, and had ordered a copy made and sent to her son. Quanah was grateful that in many ways the Indians and the Anglos were learning to trust each other.

The past could not be changed . . . but every day there was more hope for the future!

Quanah posing in Indian dress and with a painting of his mother and sister. (Smithsonian Institution Photo No. 1747-A-1)

CHAPTER 19

Wolf Hunt With "Teddy" Roosevelt

Quanah first met Theodore Roosevelt before "Teddy" became President of the United States. Roosevelt had come to Indian Territory for a reunion of his regiment of Rough Riders, a heroic fighting unit from the Spanish-American War in Cuba. The hosting committee had asked Quanah to ride in the parade and to bring along a party of young braves from the reservation. They arrived, decked out in feathers and war paint, to add color to the gala celebration.

Afterwards Quanah was introduced to the young leader from Washington. From that meeting sprang a continuing friendship, with Quanah seeing Teddy many times in the future, as well as being asked to ride in the inaugural parade when Teddy became president.

The outdoorsman president had heard about a famous wolf hunt in Indian Territory in which a Mr. Jack Abernathy would race his horse into a pack of wolves and capture one barehanded. Roosevelt was intrigued and wanted to see the event. One was scheduled to coincide with his next trip out West. Quanah's cattlemen friends obligingly set up the hunt, complete with camping equipment—including a chuck wagon— and awaited the president's arrival.

The little town of Frederick, wanting to honor Roosevelt's

THEODORE ROOSEVELT AND GROUP OF NOTED WEST TEXANS ON FAMOUS WOLF HUNT, April 1, 1905
Left to Right, Standing—Albert Bivins, Capt. Bill McDonald, Jack Abernathy, Maj. S.B. Young, Capt. S. Burk Burnett,
Col. Theodore Roosevelt, E.M. Gillis
Seated—Two Soldiers   Bonnie Mare, Chief Quanah Parker, kneeling, Cecil Lyon, 1928
                                                              R.L. Lambert, D.P. Phy Taylor.

*Quanah Parker and Teddy Roosevelt on the famous "bare-
handed wolf hunt." (Courtesy of the Panhandle-Plains
Historical Museum, Canyon, Texas)*

visit, quickly organized a parade for the occasion, and once again, Quanah would also take part in the hunt. He was asked to participate in the parade, riding alongside of the president.

Among the excited spectators was Tom Yohe, his wife and their six-year-old son, Charles. Many years later Charles—now grown, married and a grandfather himself—recalled how his father had boosted him up on his shoulders so he could see the president and the Indian chief as they rode by. "But," Yohe reminisced, "I was too young to be impressed by a president. I was more interested in the Indians and in the band music!"

The wolf hunt was conducted with the president carried along in hot pursuit of a wolf pack so he could witness, first-hand, the feat for which Abernathy had become famous. Days later, as Roosevelt prepared to return to the capital, a crowd gathered around his train, anticipating a last glimpse of the president. Roosevelt came out on the rear platform and thanked the townspeople for his nice reception. In the crowd he spotted Quanah and called the chief to come up to the platform to stand beside him. He introduced Quanah to the crowd as "my friend, the great Comanche chief!" Quanah replied with a short speech telling how he had eaten with the president in Washington, calling him the "Great White Father." Referring to him as "Big Chief to us all," Quanah earned one of Roosevelt's famous broad, toothy smiles.

The hunt so impressed the president that he returned to Washington with tales of the bravery and agility exhibited by Abernathy. When a few people scoffed, Roosevelt declared he wished he had pictures to prove his story. Motion pictures at that time were in their infancy but the president located a cameraman who agreed to film the feat for him. When the president finally received the finished short movie, he invited Quanah to a party at the White House to view the show. He presented it with a flourish, after which he introduced Quanah to his other guests, saying the chief had taken part in the film. Once again, he referred to Quanah as "The Great Comanche Chief."

CHAPTER 20

Pioneer Remembers Meeting Quanah

Young Charles Yohe, so completely enthralled by the sight of the Indians in the wolf hunt parade, certainly never expected to see the chief again. Or at such close range.

But only a week later the stage was set for just such a meeting as the Yohe family traveled toward the small town of Hobart, Indian Territory, where Tom, Charles' father, planned to set up his blacksmith shop.

Autumn was in the air, the morning crisply cool, the sparse trees on the flat landscape heralding the change of seasons with riotous colors flagging against a clear blue sky. Tom was especially grateful for the fine weather when he suddenly discovered trouble had developed along the yoke between the two mules pulling the Yohe's covered wagon. He turned the wagon off the dusty trail and headed for the small grove of oak trees a few hundred yards away. "Looks like we may be here a day or so," he told his wife regretfully after he had checked and confirmed a broken chain link.

Unhitching the mules, he staked them side by side in the patchy grass. The sun by now was almost directly overhead, warming up the autumn air. Turning to Charles, he said, "If we want any dinner today, son, we'd better get your mama a cooking fire started. How about you and me gathering up some kindling wood?"

Mrs. Yohe brought pots and pans from the wagon and put water on to boil while Tom lifted down from the wagon their rough plank table and two matching benches. Then, lacing small leafy branches between the oak trees, he made a shady arbor over their dining area. Finally he could turn his attention to the mending of the yoke.

Mrs. Yohe, opening the box that held their dinnerware, put the tin plates and cups on the table. Coffee began boiling in its pot over the fire while dried beans cooked in another. She turned out a pan of flat little biscuits, thinking all the while how nice it would be to get into town, into a house, and have a real stove to prepare their meals on again.

Charles, left to his own devices, wandered back to the wagonbed and crawled over the tailgate. Taking out his box of little wooden animals that had been his Christmas present the year before, he set them up side by side, counting the horses, the cows, the pigs, the little chickens. "One day," he thought, "I'll have my own farm. A whole herd of cattle. Work horses and horses to ride . . . " He was so engrossed in his daydreams he failed to see the Indians approaching. They were traveling along the same dusty trail the Yohes had left a short while earlier, and were still some distance away, their horses in an easy canter, when he first noticed them. Wide-eyed, Charles scrambled out of the wagon and ran to his daddy. "Indians!" he called, pointing as he ran. "Look!"

Tom paused in his labors, wiping the sweat from his brow with the back of his hand, using his arm to shade his eyes from the noonday glare. Indians, all right. There were four of them, one riding in the front. "They don't look like trouble, son," he told Charles.

Then, as the group grew closer, he said, "Well, I'll be! The big one out front looks like the chief we saw in the parade the other day."

Mrs. Yohe joined her husband and son, her heart beating

fast even though they had heard of no "Indian trouble" for some time. She watched her husband's face. He didn't seem worried. "Yeah," he said with a smile, "that's the chief all right."

Drying his hands on an old rag, he walked toward the trail along which the Indians would pass. As they drew closer he waved and called out, "Howdy! Like to come and eat with us?"

The small band followed the chief's lead, turning their horses toward Yohe. Charles, who had run along behind his father, peered at them from safety behind his father's muscular frame. The tall chief raised an arm in greeting as they approached, saying, "Me, Quanah Parker."

"I know," Tom said, extending his hand and receiving a hearty, firm grasp in return. "We saw you in the wolf hunt parade the other day, riding with Mr. Roosevelt."

Quanah dismounted, letting his reins drop. The well-trained horse stood quietly as Quanah walked away from it, back to the campsite with Tom. His eyes took in the camp scene, then scanned the area where Tom had been working. "Wagon broke?"

"Yep. 'Fraid so," Tom replied. "Just about fixed though. We should be back on the road by this time tomorrow."

Tom introduced Quanah to Mrs. Yohe and Charles before leading him to the table. Quanah took a bench on one side of the table and accepted a steaming cup of coffee from Mrs. Yohe, then ladled spoonful after spoonful of sugar into the black liquid. He smiled tolerantly and with understanding as Charles stared at him from beside his father on the opposite side of the table.

While the men talked, Mrs. Yohe set plates of boiled beans and the little biscuits before them. Quanah used the ungainly metal fork easily, sopping the remaining bean gravy from his plate with bits of bread. His braves, who had chosen to remain mounted, accepted plates of the beans and coffee, but waved away the offer of forks, instead dipping into the beans with their fingers. They spoke in Comanche as she walked back to the table.

"They say your 'little cakes' good," Quanah told her.

Later as Quanah sat astride his horse, preparing to leave, he commented, "I see Tommy have no meat to feed his family."

"No," Tom replied. "This accident just happened this morning and I haven't had time to do any hunting. Thought we'd be in town by tonight, until this happened."

Early the next morning, after a breakfast of coffee and more "little cakes" with his family, Tom reset the repaired yoke and hitched up the mules. Just then he saw the approach of the Indians again, this time coming from the opposite direction. Charles stood up on the wagon seat to get a better view, no longer intimidated by their presence. As in the past, Quanah rode ahead of the little band.

Across his saddle, swaying with the horse's movements, lay a newly butchered side of beef. Charlie watched as two of the braves dismounted and lifted the meat over the wagon's tailgate.

"Yesterday Tommy had no meat. But he shared his food with us," Quanah said briefly. "Today we share."

With a wave to the family, the Indians rode away.

CHAPTER 21

Quanah Recognized for Good Deeds

Many and varied are the tales of Quanah's savage fight against white aggression when he waged a no-holds-barred war, from the days of his early adolescence until he brought his people onto the reservation in surrender. He was the first to admit to his ferocious raids, glorying in having been a deterrent against the infringing Texans.

During a speech he made at a state fair in Dallas, Texas, in 1910 he freely admitted, "I used to be a bad man." As an instance, he recalled fighting against Colonel Mackenzie's cavalry at Blanco Canyon many years before, telling how he sent his braves to stampede horses through the camp in the middle of the night, leaving many of the cavalrymen on foot patrol the next day. "You see how bad I was at that time," he said, nonapologetically.

On the other hand, there are also many stories told about the chief by people who encountered him during those early days, and on through his reign as chief, who attest to his compassion.

It was commonly agreed that Quanah did not torture his prisoners to the death, as some Indian chiefs did. Nor did he wantonly kill women and children. His idea of war was warrior against warrior, and his tactics to force the Anglo enemy off

115

Indian lands were, more often than not, raids to steal horses which the Indians could trade to the Comancheros. These raids were meant to leave the white settlers helpless on their farm lands, in hopes they would abandon the idea of settling there. Some Indians pillaged and burned to force the white man's retreat.

One of the Anglos who could personally attest to Quanah's compassion, was Charles Yohe. It was his family Quanah befriended when Charles was just a little boy, after his father had invited the Indians to share their dinner, although the Yohes had only beans and biscuits. Many years later, Mr. Yohe, then a resident of Houston, Texas, was able to refute an ugly rumor that had persisted for years about Quanah. Yohe read an article in a magazine about an Indian chief (supposedly Quanah) who had been invited to ride in a parade in Hobart, Oklahoma, and who intended to wear a cape made of ninety-nine human scalps (many of them white!). The parade officials, when they learned of his intention, were understandably upset at the callous idea. A childhood friend of Yohe's wrote that his father had been among the delegation of officials who rode out to the chief's home and strongly advised against his wearing the cape. When the chief persisted the sheriff told him quite candidly, "I don't know if I could protect you—you'd likely be mobbed." The chief relented. Somehow through the years, the story erroneously became attributed to Quanah.

When Yohe saw the magazine article, he recalled a letter from his friend absolving Quanah of the deed, retrieved the letter from his files, and wrote the publication asking that the facts be printed, clearing Quanah's name.

As the chief became more widely traveled and better understood, his good deeds were recognized and remembered more often, and he received many honors for the role he had played as liaison between the red and white men. Among the recognitions that befell him was the naming of a town in Texas in his honor. Located in Hardeman County, roughly halfway between the Pease and Red Rivers, and later to become a county seat, the city took Quanah's name when he was about forty years old.

Shortly after the town had been established, a railroad line was built through the region. Quanah was a frequent visitor to the area, watching its progress. Taking the advice of some of his wealthy cattlemen friends, Quanah invested forty thousand dollars of his grass-rights money in the venture. In later years it was often noted how much Quanah enjoyed visiting the growing line which had become known as the Quanah, Acme and Pacific Railroad. More than once he was seen strolling through the railroad yards, patting the fat, black, puffy engine approvingly, saying, "My engine . . . my railroad!"

A commemorative celebration was held by the town nearly fifty years after his death, with a bust of the chief unveiled. Sculptured by the famed artist, Mr. Jack Hill, of Amarillo, Texas, the bust was later placed in the National Hall of Fame for Famous American Indians.

CHAPTER 22

Quanah Visits the Place of His Birth

1907

Indian tradition maintains that each person should return to the place of his birth at least once before he dies. Though Quanah had often in his lifetime been back to Laguna Sabinas, as he reached his sixties he decided he would like to make it a pilgrimage.

With several of his Indian friends in one of the new horseless carriages, he headed for West Texas. The years, he found, had wrought many changes in the area, but the valley remained flower-ladened, and sweet-smelling. He recalled how his mother had frequently reminded him, as a child, that this was where he had gotten his name.

His friends left him beside the lake for his contemplation, understanding the nature of his visit.

No longer wearing his three-piece business suit, but back to his buckskins and moccasins, he carried his rolled buffalo robe and a blanket, tobacco and his long ceremonial pipe, as he retreated up the hillside into a grove of oak and maple trees. There he spread the buffalo robe, pulled the blanket about his shoulders and sat, content in the peaceful afternoon quiet, communing with nature.

All about him he could feel Indian spirits who had long roamed the beautiful land. He relaxed and puffed on his pipe, offering it to the spirits of the east, west, north and south. With the smoke that lifted from his pipe, Quanah sent up prayers and listened for answers to waft back to him on the gentle breezes.

In his contemplation, Quanah thought of the days past. He thought of the days long before he was born, when his people had wandered this land, migrating with the seasons. And then he recalled the coming of the white settlers. He thought of the Indians' decision to fight the invaders. And he thought, too, of the cost, the lives lost on both sides.

He thought of his parents and how they had met, and why he was born, a child of two worlds. He could remember his mother's sweet face and gentle tones and loving eyes, and he thought of the last time he saw her. He thought of his father, a chief who had led his people through times of tribulation and who was taken in death while Quanah was not yet a young warrior. He thought of his younger brother and sister who were called by the Great Spirit while they were just children. He thought of his own wanderings from tribe to tribe until he was invited to join, as a young warrior, the Quahadis band, and how he eventually became their chief.

Yes, Quanah thought to himself, from that day forward I have been responsible for my people. I've done my best for their salvation. I led them in a fight to save our lands from white settlers pushing west. But when the enemy's numbers became too great, when food and clothing and housing were taken from us by the greedy hunters, I did what seemed best. I took the only way to save my people from complete annihilation by freezing and starving to death—the reservation . . .

He recalled how difficult it had been to change his ways and still remain true to his heritage. He thought of how hard it had been to make an example for his people to follow. He had promised them he would be a liaison between the red and white communities. And, Quanah concluded, I believe I have been a good one, just as I've tried to be a good chief.

Quanah spent three days alone, roaming about the hillside

The grave of Quanah's mother, Cynthia Ann Parker, Army Cemetery, Fort Sill, Oklahoma. (Smithsonian Institution Photo No. 45919)

and the valley, living in the old ways, reviewing his life. He was content that he had accomplished all he could for his people.

But there lingered in his mind one thing he had wished to do and had not. Since the day he found his mother's grave in Texas, he had wanted to have her remains and those of little Prairie Flower returned to their Comanche family just as his mother had wanted to return in life.

"That I shall do! I shall seek permission! We will be together again!" he vowed.

At the end of three days, when his companions returned for him, he approached the car with a look of contentment on his face. "It has been good," he told them, "to return to the place of my birth."

And he did fulfill that last promise to himself. He petitioned to have his mother reburied in Cache, Oklahoma, near a plot where he himself chose to be buried. Congress authorized a marble headstone quarried for his mother's grave. At her reburial Quanah spoke briefly, lovingly, reminding those who gathered in memorial how she had lived among them and loved them and been one of them.

"And now," he added, "she is home again!"

CHAPTER 23

The Chief Dies

1911

Quanah, now in his sixties, kept his spry step as he continued to look after his people's welfare. He still undertook any problem that was brought to his attention. His door was always open for friends and neighbors.

Daily he saddled his favorite horse in the corral and rode off to oversee the happenings on his lands. He still watched the brandings of new stock, often traveled to horse auctions, chose steers to add to his herd of cattle. He met with his foreman to discuss any problems that might have arisen, and was there to hand out monthly pay checks to hired hands.

Days seemed to fly by for Quanah, days as busy as ever. At the end of the year there was a fine family Christmas. Two wives, Tonarcy and Topay, still lived with Quanah in the big house that Burk Burnett had built for him, while wife Mahchee-towooky lived nearby on her own land. With all of the children borne by his wives, and now many grandchildren underfoot, Quanah happily recalled his own childhood when the tribe's grandfathers undertook his youthful training.

The new year was ushered in and Quanah began looking forward to the arrival of spring. As he did every year, he awaited the first greening of the lands. But it was early yet to be thinking of spring with anything more than an annual yearning. First

Quanah and his family in front of his house. (Courtesy of the Fort Sill Museum, Fort Sill, Oklahoma)

it was payment time at the agency, which called for a trip away from the Big House. Quanah wanted to see old friends in Hobart. He gave the trip some thought and made his decision.

Sitting on the front porch, his straight-backed chair tilted against the wall, he called Tonarcy. "It is payment time," he said. "I have to make the trip and would like to see some of our old friends along the way. Pack for both of us. We will make this a business and pleasure trip." Tonarcy was delighted. She enjoyed dressing up, taking the train, shopping in town.

During the next few days, once the agency business was behind him, Quanah and Tonarcy were able to visit friends, and to look into some of the town's stores. Quanah still enjoyed seeing his wife excited by the latest fashions and was tolerant of the few purchases she planned.

But the days of pleasure were short-lived. Quanah caught a chill and began running a fever. He became extremely ill, his temperature rising alarmingly. Tonarcy insisted they leave for home immediately, where he could be looked after by the family doctor. She telephoned ahead, making arrangements for them to be met at the station with a closed carriage. Stoically, Quanah sat through the long ride home.

The doctor who had been alerted to the situation waited at the Big House, with the family. Alarmed by the chief's appearance as he decended from the carriage, the doctor followed him to his room where Quanah's bed had been prepared, and examined him immediately. Moments later he emerged from the room with the dread diagnosis of "pneumonia!"

As Quanah lay gravely ill, he asked for his medicine man, Qua-E-I. "I must be prepared to leave this world," he told his old friend, "in true Comanche manner. Although by blood I am half-Anglo, and I have lived in both worlds, just as I asked my people never to forget their Comanche heritage, I have never forgotten mine. Speak Comanche words for my departing spirit."

With eagle feathers, Qua-E-I fanned Quanah's fevered brow. Circling the bed with the feathers held high, held low, intoning

The grave of Quanah Parker, Comanche Chief. (Courtesy of the Panhandle-Plains Historical Museum, Canyon, Texas)

special prayers for Quanah's departure from this world, he noted the chief's relaxed features, his acceptance of his coming death. Imitating the call of the great eagle, he prayed, "Father in heaven, this, our brother, is coming," and Quanah drifted peacefully away.

News of the chief's death went out by telephone and telegraph wires, with newspapers carrying his story all across the country, for Quanah had made many friends, and his reputation had spread across the nation.

He was buried in a handsome casket, in Indian dress as he had wished. A line of thousands of mourners, both red and white, filed past, paying their last respects. The funeral procession stretched for nearly two miles, out to the Post Oak Mission Cemetery at Cache, Oklahoma, where Quanah was laid to rest alongside his mother's grave.

In 1930, by special appropriation of Congress, the small original headstone was replaced by a tall granite tombstone which reads:

RESTING HERE UNTIL DAY BREAKS
AND SHADOWS FALL AND DARKNESS
DISAPPEARS IS
QUANAH PARKER
LAST CHIEF OF THE COMANCHES

Epilogue

For nearly forty-five years Quanah rested as he had wished, beside his mother and little sister, in the Post Oak Mission Cemetery in Cache, Oklahoma.

Then Fort Sill found it necessary to expand its artillery range and needed those burial grounds.

Quanah was reinterred at the Army Cemetery at Fort Sill, a Comanche hero alongside U.S. Army heros. Hundreds of people attended the reburial, including Quanah's last surviving widow, Topay, who was then eighty-seven years of age.

In 1953, almost forty-two years after Quanah's death, the first reunion of his red and white descendants was held.

It was through Quanah's influence that his two worlds had been brought together in friendship.

Now, almost forty years later, the reunions are still held, one year in Fort Parker, Texas, where Quanah's story really began, and the next year in Cache, Oklahoma, where he is buried.

The families gather to exchange pictures and memories; plays are presented depicting the Parker saga.

It is in reverence engendered by the chief's memory that the descendants of his red and white heritage gather to celebrate the love and friendship Quanah initiated among them during his tenure as the last great Comanche chief.

Glossary

Comancheros (co man CHAIR os)—traders who came from the northern part of Mexico into Comanche territory to trade guns and ammunition in return for the horses and cattle stolen by the Indians from Texas settlers

Esa-tai (ay sah TIE)—medicine man for Quanah's Quahadis band who erroneously predicted a victory for the Indians at the Battle of Adobe Walls

Laguna Sabinas (lah GOON ah sah BEAN us)—a salt lake centered in a flower-filled valley variously described as being near the present town of Lamesa, Texas and Seminole, Texas

Llano Estacado, or Staked Plains (YA no es tah CAH doe)—great grass-covered plains stretching through West Texas from the Red River at the Oklahoma border, south almost to Mexico

Naudah (NAH dah)—mother of Quanah. The Comanche name given to Cynthia Ann Parker after her capture and later adoption into their tribe

Peta Nocona (PAYtah no CO nah)—chief of the Noconis band of Comanches and father of Quanah

Qua-E-I (quah E I)—medicine man who sent Comanche prayers for Quanah as he lay dying

Quahadis (quah HA dees)—a band of Comanches whom Quanah eventually joined and led after the capture of his mother by the Anglos and the death of his father

Quanah (QUAH nah)—son of Cynthia Ann Parker and Chief Peta Nocona

Travois (trav WAH)—two long poles fastened one on each side of a horse or mule with the back ends of the poles dragging along the ground. Between these poles household goods were strung, to facilitate moving from camp to camp

Wives of Quanah Parker:

Ta-ho-yea (Apache—this marriage did not last. She returned to her people with Quanah's blessings)
Weckeah
Chony
Mahcheetowooky
Aerwuthtakeum
Coby
Topay
Tonarcy

Credits

Page 1 of Introduction—Information on Comanche tribe from *The Old West: The Great Chiefs,* by the editors of Time-Life Books, with text by Benjamin Capps. Copyright © 1975 Time-Life Books, Inc.

Page 29—Information regarding naming ceremony from *The Indians of Texas from Prehistoric to Modern Times,* by W.W. Newcomb, Jr., University of Texas Press, Austin, Texas 1961

Page 43—Information regarding interpreter from *Quanah, the Eagle of the Comanches,* by Zoe A. Tilghman, Harlow Publishing Company, Oklahoma City, Oklahoma 1938

Page 53—Information on Quanah's first wife—Ibid.

Pages 58-60—Quotes from Lieutenant Carter from *Death Song: The Last of the Indian Wars,* by John Edward Weems, Doubleday and Company, Inc., Garden City, N.Y.

Page 73—Details on attack on Indians from *Quanah, the Eagle of the Comanches,* by Zoe A. Tilghman, Harlow Publishing Company, Oklahoma City, Oklahoma 1938

Page 79—Quanah's quote from *Death Song: The Last of the Indian Wars,* by John Edward Weems, Doubleday and Company, Inc., Garden City, N.Y.

Pages 82-83—Quanah's quote—Ibid.

Page 93—Information on Quanah's home—Ibid.

Page 103—Information on gas incident from *The Last Captive*, by A.C. Greene, The Encino Press, Austin, Texas 1972

Pages 104-105—Story of picture of Quanah's mother from *Quanah, the Eagle of the Comanches*, by Zoe A. Tilghman, Harlow Publishing Company, Oklahoma City, Oklahoma 1938

Pages 111-114—Story of meeting with Quanah from personal letter, Charles W. T. Yohe, dated June 11, 1987

Page 116—Rumor of Quanah's scalp cape—Ibid.

Page 122—General information taken from *Quanah, the Eagle of the Comanches*, by Zoe A. Tilghman, Harlow Publishing Company, Oklahoma City, Oklahoma 1938

Bibliography

Anderson, LaVere. *Quanah Parker: Indian Warrior for Peace.* Champaign, Illinois: Garrard Publishing Co., 1973.

Capps, Benjamin F. "The Two Lives of Quanah Parker," *The Old West: The Great Chiefs.* Alexandria, West Virginia: Time-Life Books, 1975.

Carter, Capt. R.G. *On the Border With MacKenzie.* New York: Antiquarian Press, Ltd., 1961.

De Shields, James T. "The Fall of Parker's Fort." Extract from *Border Wars of Texas.*

Fehrenbach, T.R. *Lone Star: A History of Texas and the Texans.* New York: Macmillan Co., 1968.

Greene, A.C. *The Last Captive.* Austin, Texas: Encino Press, 1972.

Jackson, Clyde L. and Grace. *Quanah Parker: Last Chief of the Comanches.* New York: Exposition Press.

Life of Quanah Parker, Comanche Chief, By His Son, Chief Baldwin Parker, through J. Evetts Haley, Indiahoma, Oklahoma: Aug. 1930.

May, Julian. *Quanah, Leader of the Comanches,* 1970.

Newcomb, William W. *The Indians of Texas: From Prehistoric to Modern Times.* Austin: University of Texas Press, 1967.

O'Quinn, Eugene, personal letter, Sept. 26, 1983.

Poor's Railroad Manual: Railroads of the U.S., addenda. New York, 1910.

Richardson, Rupert N. "Cynthia Ann Parker." *Women of Texas Magazine,* Waco, Texas: Texian Press, 1972.

Selden, Jack. "On the Trail of Cynthia Ann Parker," *Texas Highways Magazine,* 1983.

Wallace, Ernest and Hoebel, E. Adamson. *The Comanches: Lords of the South Plains.* Norman: University of Oklahoma Press, 1952.

Weems, John Edward. *Death Song: The Last of the Indian Wars.* Garden City, New York, 1952.

Yohe, Charles W.T., personal letter, 1987.